THE ENCHANTED WORLD OF HONEY MOON

A SCARY LITTLE CHRISTMAS

by
Regina Jennings

Created by Mark Andrew Poe

Illustrations by Christina Weidman

rabbit publishers

A Scary Little Christmas (The Enchanted World of Honey Moon),
by Regina Jennings
Created by Mark Andrew Poe

Rabbit Publishers
1624 W. Northwest Highway
Arlington Heights, IL 60004

Illustrations by Christina Weidman
Cover and Interior Design by Lewis Design & Marketing

ISBN: 978-1-943785-06-3

10 9 8 7 6 5 4 3 2 1

1. Fiction - Action and Adventure 2. Children's Fiction
First Edition
Printed in U.S.A.

I go where I am needed.

~ HONEY MOON

TABLE OF CONTENTS

PREFACE

Halloween visited the little town of Sleepy Hollow and never left. Many moons ago, a sly and evil mayor found the powers of darkness helpful in building Sleepy Hollow into "Spooky Town," one of the country's most celebrated attractions. Now, years later, the indomitable Honey Moon is choosing to make life difficult for the mayor and his evil associates.

Welcome to *The Enchanted World of Honey Moon*. Halloween may have found a home in Sleepy Hollow, but Honey and her friends are going to make sure it doesn't stay forever.

THE VILE DELIVERY

Honey Moon stood on the stage and slowly spun her shepherd's staff like a ninja ready to attack. The parts for the annual Christmas pageant had already been assigned and changing Mrs. Psalter's mind was harder than Algebra. But that didn't keep Honey from trying.

"Sure, it'd be nice if Becky and I could both play the role of Mary," Honey said. "But since I've already memorized the lines, it only seems right that you switch the roles. Becky will do fine as a shepherd."

Her best friend Becky nodded in agreement. "Honey has never gotten to be Mary, and I was it last year. And she does have the lines memorized."

And that's why they were best friends—because Becky, even with her only slightly-above-average intelligence, was a reasonable person, which was rare as far as ten-year-old girls went. Come to think of it, reasonable people were a rarity, no matter what their age.

Take Mrs. Psalter for an example. How could she stick Honey in such an unimportant role? Shepherds were boring. The Moon family's fireplace manger scene had been missing the shepherd for years and no one even cared, or noticed. Which was good because Honey distinctly remembered the 4th of July when thanks to a science experiment she was conducting, the shepherd rode the Dynamo-Exploding Patriotic Rocket bound to glory. But if they lost the Mary figurine, the whole nativity set would have to be replaced. Which is exactly why Honey thought she should have the starring role. Someone with her intellect should be wearing the pretty blue gown instead of the rough shepherd clothes.

"No," Mrs. Psalter said to Becky. "You are perfect for Mary." Mrs. Psalter had a big face, but she kept her eyes, nose and mouth all crammed together in the center of it. "You have beautiful dark, curly hair—"

"Mary could have had blond hair, couldn't she?" Honey flipped a tangled ponytail over her shoulder. "Or I could wear a wig."

But Mrs. Psalter shook her head. "Becky will be Mary because Mary was gracious, and kind, and merciful. Mary did not argue, or interrupt adults to tell them they were wrong and how they should be directing the play.

4

Becky is nice, and for this role a kind heart is more important than being a know-it-all."

Mrs. Psalter's son, Scooter, who was tall, handsome and in eighth grade, put his homework down, stood up in the front row, and clapped his hands. The smacks echoed loudly across the empty sanctuary. Honey lowered her shepherd's staff and wiggled her toes. They wouldn't treat her brother Harry with this kind of disrespect.

"Shepherds rule," Honey muttered even though she didn't quite mean it. She looked at Becky. "You'll learn your lines," she said. "I'll help you."

"Excuse me, am I in the right place?" Honey and Becky both turned around. There was a tall, husky man in brown clothes carrying some kind of electronic gadget.

"Not unless you like bad singing and lame costumes," Scooter said.

Eighth-graders didn't have to be in the play. That's why he could sit and make fun of them.

Mrs. Psalter clomped off the stage in her heavy winter boots. "Can I help you, young man? We are in the middle of our Christmas rehearsal."

"Christmas rehearsal? Perfect." The delivery man punched some buttons on his electronic clipboard. "I'll be right back."

"Did we order new costumes?" asked Brianna. She'd already hot-glued sequins all over her angel costume and when those ran out she started using empty foil candy wrappers. The girl was strange. If only Honey could get away with the stuff Brianna did.

"No new costumes," Mrs. Psalter said. "I can't imagine what he might have."

The delivery man pushed the church door open and carried in a giant Santa Claus. "Had to take it out of the box," he said, "to fit through the door." But when he set it on its feet and turned it around, the kids all gasped. Santa had red, angry eyes. Vampire fangs stuck out of his beard, and his sack of toys had been replaced with a pitchfork held in blood-splattered gloves.

"Get that monster out of here!" Mrs. Psalter said.

The delivery man scratched his head. "What do you want us to do with the rabid reindeer?"

The door opened again and a second delivery man walked in carrying a life-sized plastic reindeer that looked more like a were-wolf than Rudolph. "This here is Slasher. Mag-got, Cujo and the rest are still in the truck."

Honey looked at her sock-covered feet. She had a low nightmare threshold. In plain words, that meant that anything creepy, weird or scary could give her nightmares worse than the elevator prank video on YouTube. She had to look away. Pretend she was somewhere nice. Like her kitchen at home. Feeding Jell-O to her little brother Harvest.

Becky left the spotlight and came to the dark part of the stage to stand next to Hon-ey. "Remember that time we fed lime Jell-O to Harvest and he smeared it in his hair?" she asked. "That was so funny."

Becky deserved the best part in the play.

Even if she couldn't spell *perpendicular,* she was a good friend.

Mrs. Psalter was not yelling. She said she never yelled. But she was using her lungs at one-hundred percent. "Those do not belong here! Remove them at once!"

The first man looked at his clipboard. "Oh, this is North Church. I bet these go to the big tent next door. That must be where the Haunted Holiday Festival is."

Haunted Holiday Festival? Honey sure didn't know anything about a Haunted Holiday Festival, but she was sick and tired of all the Halloween stuff in her town—Sleepy Hollow, Massachusetts. A Haunted Holiday Festival must be something new for Sleepy Hollow, whose motto was: Where Every Day is Halloween Night. Where all the stores had creepy names like The Witching Hour Candy Store and Screaming Jelly Bean. Where the local radio station played Thriller, Ghostbusters, and Monster Mash all year. But Honey didn't want a scary, merry Christmas. No, Honey wanted her town to have a normal

Christmas, not one with cobwebs and dripping fangs attached.

Sleepy Hollow where even Santa Claus could give a smart ninja shepherd nightmares.

GREAT EXPECTATIONS

The Moon family mini-van smelled like French fries. Honey closed the door behind her and buckled up.

"How was practice?" Mary Moon asked.

"Did Becky remember her lines? There weren't any kings getting choked on their capes this time were there?" She turned to look over her shoulder. "No, no, Harvest. Only one fry. You have to share."

"I wish we could have a normal, traditional Christmas for once," said Honey. She folded her arms across her chest and looked out the window. "A fun celebration with old time music instead of all the weird Halloween stuff that goes on in town."

"What are you talking about?" her mother asked.

Honey caught her mother's eye in the rearview mirror. "Do you know what would be awesome? What if our Christmas play was about the cosmic battle going on? What if angels had to protect the baby from these dark forces that were trying to hurt him? I bet it happened. And the angels wouldn't be in white robes, but in armor. Shining armor. They'd be tough and they wouldn't be afraid of any scary reindeer or vampire Santa Claus."

She'd said too much. Honey's mom fixed her with that *I'm-about-to-learn-your-secrets-and-you-are-powerless-to-stop-me* look. "What's this about a vampire Santa?"

They'd stopped at the corner of the park next to the church. The big black tent sat on the back part. Mounds of dirty snow squatted where the snow plows had left them.

"Do you know about the Haunted Holiday Festival?" Honey asked.

"Yes, we're having it right there." Mary flipped her turn signal while nodding toward the field. "But I didn't know we were having a vampire Santa."

"Well I saw him—fangs and all. And...and who's we?"

"The town, I guess. I haven't heard any names, come to think of it, and nothing about a planning committee."

And that was a bad sign.

Sleepy Hollow used to be just a regular town. Sure, with a name like Sleepy Hollow, people were always going to have their laughs. Honey Moon understood embarrassing names. But over the last few years, the town had changed. The mayor and Selectmen decided to make money on their funny name. Instead of telling visitors the truth, that the Sleepy Hollow they were looking for was in New York and sending them on their way, they decided to become the spooky town from Washington Irving's famous story. And it worked. Tourists flocked to town, making money for everyone. Soon storefronts were filled with eerie displays. Fake cobwebs hung from every ceiling. Skeletons and bubbling cauldrons were everywhere. Almost no public place was safe from the dark decorations.

The main attraction was the horrifying, bronze statue of the famous Headless Horseman that crackled with evil. It stood right smack dab in the center of the town green like Mr. Headless was a war hero or something. People flocked to it to take selfies, but Honey would rather look away every time they passed it.

14

"They are going to decorate the tent with scary Christmas decorations," Honey said. "They even have rabid reindeer." She shuddered.

"The tourists will love it, but I have to agree with you on this one." Mary tapped the steering wheel. "Why can't Mayor Kligore just let Christmas be about good, not darkness? When I was a girl, I loved the pretty lights on Christmas. I especially loved the bells in the church steeple. They'd ring and ring, for hours it seemed."

15

"Bells? What bells?" Honey asked.

"The church bells, of course," said her mom as she turned the wheel and headed toward Shopper's Row. "They were amazing! Just think, Honey. High up in the church belfry were twelve bells, some bigger than the others to make different notes, but they were all cast in bronze and positively gorgeous in their ages-old patina. Twelve people would stand under them and pull the ropes that were attached to the wheels that turned—"

"Sounds complicated," Honey said.

"Not really. It's physics. Anyway, the ringers would pull the ropes which made the headstock move which made the bells swing and produce beautiful music. The ringers all had to be in perfect time. It was really quite a feat. And once they were going, you couldn't get away from them. They filled the air, echoing their joyous strains.
"

Honey looked in the side mirror of the mini-van. The church steeple was behind them now, but even at night the white spire glowed. It shone, but it was as silent as the graveyard.

"I wish they'd ring again," Honey said. "Maybe then people would want to come to our play. It would be like history in the making."

Harvest let go a juicy French fry burp.

"Say excuse me, Harvest," Mary said.

Harvest giggled.

"I just want people to come to the play. We worked really hard and even though I still think that I'd be a better Mary, Becky is really trying hard and it wouldn't be right, Mom, you know if—"

"If no one came?"

"Yeah. Because of the Haunted Holiday Festival." Honey sighed. She would have to find a way. She would save Christmas!

17

Honey was surprised when they pulled up to The Bride of Frankenstein store. Bride of Frankenstein sold old-fashioned, white wedding dresses if you asked for one, but the window display contained a black gown with gray, lacy sleeves that looked like spider webs. In fact, when Honey looked closer she could see that the lace had been tatted to look like spiders. She shook her head.

"What are we doing here?" Honey asked. "Who's getting married?"

"They sell more than wedding clothes,"

her mother said. "You can order formal clothes of all kinds here. And besides, Honey, you should know not to ask about shopping trips at Christmastime. Let me have some secrets."

Her mother split some more fries between Honey and Harvest. "I'll be right back," she said. "Don't look when you see me coming. It might ruin someone's Christmas."

As soon as the car doors were locked, Honey set her brain to figuring out exactly what gift her mother had ordered. At Chez Moon, the Moon children only got one present each on Christmas Eve. Sure they bought each other something if they had allowance, or sometimes they made something, but from their parents they only got one gift. Usually it was the best and most terrific gift Harry, Honey, and even Harvest, who was finally catching on to Christmas, could ever imagine. Last year, Honey got a black and yellow bike with a striped bee-seat. It had a horn on it that squawked loud, and there was a custom license plate that said HONEYBEE. That was the best gift ever.

18

So what could mom be getting at a wedding dress shop?

Honey handed Harvest an extra-long French fry, then closed her eyes and imagined with all her imagining strength. She imagined the most beautiful dress in the world. It would be yellow, but not short like little girls wear. It would be long, like a prom dress. And it wouldn't be too sparkly, not like Brianna's sequined angel dress. And when she wore it, all her big brother's friends wouldn't think she was a snotty, know-it-all. They would think she was a pretty young lady. And they would sit still and look at her when she talked, just like they did Sarah Sinclair.

It was such a perfect Christmas present that Honey was surprised she hadn't already thought of it. She was ten-years-old. Of course, it was time she had a formal dress of her own. She felt practically giddy at the thought.

When her mom came out of the store, Honey covered her eyes like she was supposed to. But from between her fingers she saw a flash of yellow hanging out from the bottom of the garment bag.

This would be the best Christmas ever!

Sing-a-Ring-a-Ling

M iss Fortissimo was the choir teacher at Sleepy Hollow Elementary. She loved long necklaces just like she loved long notes. Today, her necklace stretched lower than her belly button. It rattled against the piano keys as she bent to play the tune that meant, STOP TALKING AND LISTEN TO YOUR

TEACHER. No one ever stopped talking when they heard those notes. Ever.

She reached for the bullhorn that hung by the flag. Miss Fortissimo claimed it was a last resort, but she last-resorted three times a day. "QUIET!" she yelled through the horn. "And I mean it."

The students settled down and stopped talking.

22

"That's better," Miss Fortissimo said. She replaced the bullhorn on its hook. Then she leaned against the back of the piano and smiled. "We have an exciting opportunity, class. The Sleepy Hollow Elementary choir has been invited to sing at the Haunted Holiday Festival on Christmas Eve. The whole town will be there."

A couple of kiss-up girls clapped and huddled together with excited whispers. Honey rolled her eyes.

"But what about the Christmas play?" Honey asked. "It's on Christmas Eve, too. Why would anyone want to go somewhere spooky on Christmas?"

The girls snickered and whispered louder. Jacob Norman laughed. "Because it's funner than some dumb play."

"Blockhead," Honey said. "Funner is not a word."

Miss Fortissimo glared at Honey. "That's enough, Honey Moon." Some kids chuckled like they often did when someone used Honey's full name. But she didn't care. The Christmas pageant was far more important.

"I'm talking to Mrs. Psalter about canceling the play," Miss Fortissimo said. "The festival is going to be spectacular. I personally rewrote some Christmas songs to better fit with the theme." She cleared her throat and began singing while waving her hand in the air:

"Silver Bells, Scary Tales, it's winter time in Sleepy Hollow,

Ring-a-ling, hear them scream, soon it will be frightening...."

Honey thought of the vampire Santa and got that fluttery feeling in her tummy again. But the feeling only made her more determined to keep the play alive. "But the Christmas program is going to be better than any haunted festival."

"What's so great about your Christmas play? Do you have scary elves? Or a vampire Santa," asked a smelly boy from class.

Honey hadn't even thought about the evil elves and scary reindeer. Sure, guys like Jacob Norman and those silly girls would love that, but she couldn't let the Christmas play get canceled, because that would mean NO normal celebration and she would be forced to sing with the school choir. And that meant she would have to attend the haunted festival. UGH! She had to tell them the church had something even better planned. *Think fast, Honey Moon.*

"We don't have stupid elves. We have something even better," she said. "Something splendiferous."

"Better than poisonous mistletoe?" That was Clair Sinclair, Sarah's little sister. Claire had straight, short, blond hair that was usually hidden under a baseball cap. Today she had on a Celtics jersey over a long-sleeved T-shirt and stylishly ripped blue jeans. Claire wasn't the type to like choir, but since they wouldn't let her sign up for gym class twice a day, she'd had no choice.

25

"Mistletoe is poisonous," Honey said, but she was losing their attention. She needed to come up with something spectacular. Something earthshaking. Something they couldn't resist. "Bells," she blurted. "We have bells."

Miss Fortissimo hooked her thumb in her necklace. The chain made white marks on her neck. "What are you talking about?" she asked.

Most of the class laughed. "Who cares about dumb bells?" Aiden said. Then he snorted like a pig and said, "Hey, I made a joke. Get it? Dumbbells like weightlifters..."

"Yes, yes, we get it." But even Miss Fortissimo couldn't contain a snicker.

Honey pointed upward as if the bell tower was right above them. "The bells in the tower. Loud bells. Bells that rattle your bones more than any fake vampire Santa. Bells that squeeze your heart and shake your soul. Bells that are magical." She added the magical part for good measure.

Miss Fortissimo squinted at her. "I've lived here five years and I've never heard bells in our town. Not those kind of bells."

"You will on Christmas Eve," Honey said. "But that's only if we have the Christmas play. Otherwise there won't be any reason to ring them."

"I saw a picture of the Liberty Bell in Washington, D.C.," Claire said.

"The Liberty Bell is in Philadelphia," Honey corrected.

"But it was epic," Claire continued. "I bet a bell like that would rattle your teeth. Even with a crack in it."

"There are twelve bells, to be precise," Honey said. "And it takes twelve people to ring them. Twelve people who have to work together in perfect harmony. It's not easy."

The murmurs were divided between excitement for the Haunted Holiday Festival and the long-silent bells. Miss Fortissimo was not happy.

"The Haunted Festival is so boring. Same old Sleepy Hollow stuff," Honey continued. "But the ringing of the bells at Old North for the first time in years is . . . is history." Honey stood and placed her hand over her heart. "History. Like the signing of the Declaration of Independence. Like the first astronaut to walk on the moon. Like apple pie and — "

28

"Baseball," said Claire.

"That's right," Honey said.

That was when the class erupted with everyone talking. It sounded like a zoo had gone crazy. Miss Fortissimo snagged the bullhorn again.

"Class," she said into the horn. "Class. CLASS!"

Everyone settled. Honey had gotten so excited she had to wipe some sweat from her forehead. Maybe, just maybe she made her point. Except . . . except now she had to deliver on her promise.

Miss Fortissimo sat at the piano. "If the Christmas program gets canceled, Honey, I expect to see you at the festival. Don't forget, it'll also count as extra credit."

The day Honey needed extra credit in choir was the day she withdrew her membership from the genius club. Still, she had her way out. Unless Mrs. Psalter canceled, Honey would snatch at least one holiday away from the Headless Horseman and the ghouls of Sleepy Hollow.

29

30

MUNITY

oney hunched her shoulders and hurried past the Haunted Holiday Festival tent on her way to play practice. It was chilly and the sky was clouding up like maybe rain was on the way.

"Hey, Honey. Whatcha doing?" Noah yelled.

"You gotta come see this stuff. It's sick!"

Normally Honey would've chatted, but she kept running. Noah was okay as far as boys went, but Honey got chills thinking about the scary stuff in that tent. Besides, after the scene she made at school, she should probably stay away from the place.

Once inside the auditorium, she unwrapped her yellow and white striped scarf and hung her coat on the pegs along the wall. Practice hadn't started yet, but everyone was getting into place. The little boy playing the cow was sitting on the steps of the stage, picking his nose and wiping boogers on the blanket in the manger. The innkeeper had his costume hiked up and was playing "hot lava" in the aisle, trying to keep his feet on the hymnals he'd scattered on the ground. Becky was helping Brianna untangle her hair from the jewels she'd added to her costume.

Brianna was always getting into these messes. But just when you thought she needed a full-time babysitter, she'd do something brilliant. Even now she had that spaced-out look on her face that she wore half the time. The look that said something she was thinking was a whole lot more interesting than you were.

Honey found her shepherd costume lying on a table with a couple of other angel dresses and two leftover halos. That's when she saw the three Wise Men walk up to Mrs. Psalter looking like they'd lost their camels.

"We're going to the Haunted Holiday Festival. That's where everyone is going," the Wise Men informed Mrs. Psalter. They spoke in unison. Honey pulled her shepherd's costume over her blue sweater and plaid skirt. *Pretty sure they rehearsed that.*

Mrs. Psalter's eyebrows lowered, making the features of her face more crowded. "But how are we going to do the play without the Wise Men?"

"Cancel it," Balthazar said. "Or let Scooter take a part."

"No, way!" Scooter fell back against the pew. "It's bad enough that Mom makes me come watch practice every night."

"And we want to keep the costumes until after Christmas," said Melchior. "These king costumes make great wizard outfits."

Mrs. Psalter was speechless. She glanced over a Honey. Honey did her best imitation of her father's nod of encouragement.

Balthazar nodded, but he didn't look encouraging. More like a bobble-head doll. "Everyone will be dressed up, and there'll be food trucks with burgers and fries and funnel cakes. Way better than juice and cookies."

The other kids cheered. "Funnel cakes! Hooray!"

Honey spun her shepherd's staff wishing she could whack a wise man. Everyone couldn't quit. She didn't want to be the only one not going to the Haunted Holiday Festival.

Claire walked in. Her hair was in a short ponytail. She stood just inside the door, with her hands in her pockets, and cut a whistle so stout that the pipes on the organ rang. The auditorium went silent. The whistle even got Brianna's attention.

35

"Who's in charge here?" Claire asked in a voice more appropriate for coaching soccer.

Mrs. Psalter's little eyes expanded. "I am, and whistling is not welcome here, young lady."

With a shrug, Claire marched down the aisle to face Mrs. Psalter. The Wise Men parted like they were the Red Sea. "I'm here to ring the bells," Claire said.

Honey covered her mouth. Oh no. Disaster.

"The bells?" Mrs. Psalter frowned. "There are no bells in this program." She shooed the wise men away.

Becky raised her hand. "She's talking about the church bells. You know, the ones in the steeple."

Mrs. Psalter frowned even more. Honey inched forward. "This is my fault. I haven't exactly got permission about the bells yet."

"Honey Moon, are you trying to rewrite my script again?" Mrs. Psalter asked. "One more attempt at undermining my authority and I will ban you from the performance. Or worse, I'll make you be a cow with Roger. And he needs a tissue."

"So there aren't going to be any bells?" Claire

looked at Honey. "You fibbed!"

"Honey," Becky said, "you didn't make that up, did you? What you said in school?"

"It's true. There are bells," Honey said. "I just...I just hadn't asked if we could ring them yet."

Claire pointed to the table full of shepherd staffs and halos. "I don't want to be in any hokey play unless I get to do something cool like ring the bells."

Honey knew the feeling. She plucked at the ugly shepherd's robe. "What if I talked to Reverend Allen? He might agree to let us ring the bells."

"He's on sabbatical, getting ready for the holiday season. The play will be perfect without bells," said Mrs. Psalter. "And besides only the church secretary knows where he is and he left strict orders not to be disturbed except for an emergency."

"Look, Mrs. Psalter," Honey said, "you need something to make this play more important than the festival. With all that noise outside, who is going to come in the church? We need the bells. We need to make history. Otherwise we are wasting our time."

Mrs. Psalter wasn't cooperating. Honey needed to sweeten the deal. Her eyes darted around the kids and costumes and scenery looking for a clue. Something she could bargain with. Then she saw him. Scooter. Scooter Psalter doing his homework on the front row. He grimaced so hard it looked like he had just sucked ten lemons. She took a deep breath, and prepared to make the ultimate sacrifice. "Here's what I'll do. In return for you letting us ring the bells, I'll help Scooter with his essay after practice."

Scooter's head popped up. "I don't need help from some fifth-grader, especially a girl."

Honey sighed. He was so cute. And she was so toast.

Mrs. Psalter took a deep breath and blew it out her tiny nose. "You don't even know how to find the Reverend. He's at a retreat. And what if he says no?"

"I'll help Scooter, anyway."

"Will not!" But his tough guy act was failing. "Mom, please. Don't make me. I can do this myself."

Mrs. Psalter scratched the mole on her jaw. "It's a deal. As long your friend here participates, bells or no bells."

Honey turned to Claire. Claire rolled her eyes. "Whatever."

And that was as close to a yes as they would get. Honey would get to hear the bells, but only if she could convince Reverend Allen, and she didn't even know where he was. But more importantly she would have a chance at a normal Christmas, for once in her life.

After practice Honey, Becky and Claire, who'd invited herself, walked to Burger Heaven for milkshakes and fries.

"I can't believe you get to work with Scooter." Becky paused for another sip of her peppermint shake. "He's in eighth grade!"

40

"And he's good at baseball," added Claire. Becky and Honey often stopped at Burger Heaven before walking home. Just the two of them. But since Claire was now in the play, there wasn't anything Honey could do about keeping her away.

"I don't think you understand the sacrifice I'm making," said Honey. She ran her finger along the tabletop like she was doing a business presentation. "First off, Scooter is cute. True, he's a cootie-laden boy, but I know from watching everyone else in our species that I will outgrow that opinion, so looking to the future."

"You call that a sacrifice?" Becky asked.

"I'm not finished," Honey said. "Second, as cute as he may be, he is a pain in the rear. Working with him will not be pleasant. And third, I can't rewrite the paper for him, that would be academically dishonest, and yet it I have to make it good enough that I won't be shamed if anyone hears that I'm the one who helped him."

"Blah, blah, blah," said Claire. "Get to the point." She pulled the straw from her chocolate banana shake and licked the ice cream off.

Honey narrowed her eyes. "Middle school boys cannot admit a girl is smarter than they are, especially one who's younger. By tutoring

41

him, I will forever be blacklisted. He will hate my guts with all his heart."

Becky looked near tears. "I'm so sorry. I never thought of it that way. We don't have to do the bells."

"Too late," Claire exclaimed. "She promised. And now I have a plan to find this referee that you're looking for."

"Do you mean Reverend?" Becky asked. "It's okay. I get confused, too."

"It's my plan," said Honey. "I'm the leader here."

Claire laughed. "You're the leader? What teams are you captain of again?"

"I don't do teams," said Honey, "because I don't need a lot of people getting in my way."

Becky looked hurt. Claire flipped her ponytail over her shoulder. "Then me and Becky will just go to the Haunted Holiday Festival on Christmas Eve, if that's what you want. Besides, this sounds like it's going to take a lot of sleuthing. I don't know that you have it in you. Not without our help."

Honey's fist clenched. Did anyone like Claire and her smart mouth? The way she argued and interrupted people to tell them what they were doing wrong. Sometimes being kind-hearted was more important than being a know-it-all.

"I can sleuth," Honey said. "I can sleuth with the best of them. Just call me Sherlock."

43

"Oh yeah? What are you getting for Christmas . . . Sherlock?"

Honey leaned over the table and crumpled a napkin in her fist. "I already know."

"What is it?"

"I'm not telling."

"You don't know," Claire said.

"Do too," said Honey.

"Then tell." Claire leaned back against the thick-cushioned booth.

Becky hated conflict. She studied the French fries like she was trying to decide which was the greasiest.

"It's from Bride of Frankenstein," Honey said. "Mom told me to close my eyes when she came out of the store with it, but I peeked. It's yellow, it's satin and I'm going to look beautiful in it and that's all I'm saying."

"Only Scooter Psalter won't speak to you anymore, so what's it matter?" Claire laughed.

"Claire," Becky said. "The bells are Honey's idea, so don't you think she should be the leader?"

Claire made a loud slurping noise through her straw. Then she pinned Honey with a burning look. "We'll see how she does."

Honey sunk into the booth and sipped on her milkshake. Was Claire now officially part of the gang? How had things gone so wrong?

44

ON THE HOME FRONT

"I'll see if he can make an appearance." Mary Moon held her cell phone between her shoulder and her ear while she bathed Harvest in the kitchen sink. "His schedule is pretty full, but he loves visiting the kids at the hospital."

Honey dropped her ratty book bag on the table. Her father John Moon followed her inside and opened the refrigerator to grab a *Boost 109* energy drink.

"I'm not going to make it 'til bedtime if I don't get some caffeine," he said.

Honey grimaced as he drank the nasty-tasting stuff. She knew because he once let Honey take a sip. She thought it tasted like gym socks soaked in green cough syrup.

"I wanna drink," Harvest said.

"What are you doing in the sink?" Honey asked. "Aren't you too big?"

"It's a secret," he said.

Mary signaled in mom-sign-language to keep their voices down. "Yes," she said into the phone. "He's a special boy, that's for sure." She dumped a bowl of water over Harvest's head to rinse the soap out, still clutching the phone against her ear. "I appreciate you saying that. We are very proud of him."

Obviously Mom was talking about Honey's big brother. Harry Moon had lived a remarkable life in his thirteen years. Magician, warrior, fighter of darkness — he was doing important stuff. She, on the other hand, was dressing like a shepherd and tutoring Scooter Psalter.

"Where's Harry?" Honey mouthed.

Her mother ended the call with her thumb and dumped another bowl of water on Harvest. "To answer all of the questions that couldn't wait until my conversation was finished — Harvest is in the sink because he wanted to make a yogurt mishmash. He opened all the different flavors of yogurt and mixed them together . . . in my purse. It was easier to throw him in the sink and not risk dripping yogurt all over the house. It was all I could do to keep Half Moon from giving him a bath for me. That dog! As if I needed one more thing to deal with."

Honey knew her mother was frustrated, but

47

she couldn't help but laugh. "That would've been awesome."

Mary frowned as she pulled the plug on the sink and grabbed a towel. "Now I'm late picking Harry up from Declan's. Could this day get any crazier?"

"What's for dinner?" Dad asked.

Mom narrowed her eyes.

48

"I'll order pizza," he said.

She handed him the towel. "Thank you."

"And take my keys," he said. "They are yogurt free."

A quick kiss and she was gone.

John turned to Harvest, shivering in the empty sink. "C'mon boy. Let's get you warmed up." He wrapped him in the towel and lifted him out. "Honey, grab him some clean clothes out of the laundry room, please."

Mom had been putting in a lot of hours at her job as a nurse at Massachusetts General lately, which meant clean clothes didn't always make it to the closets and drawers. In fact the laundry room was a good place for stashing everything. Honey had just lifted a pair of clean pajamas off the ironing board when she spotted something bright and new in the cabinet above the dryer. Something that she'd never seen before. Something in a bag. It must be a present. If she was going to be a super sleuth she should know not just what she was getting for Christmas, but what everyone in the family would get, too. It'd make good practice and shut Claire up, too. *Way to go, Sherlock.*

Honey pushed her hair behind her ear and opened the door to the dryer. Then she stepped on the edge of the dryer drum and climbed on top of the machine. She paused as she heard her dad carry Harvest into the living room. She had to be very careful. Honey's knees dug into the top of the dryer as she stretched to reach the cabinet door. She opened the door and grabbed the bag. It was big. The colors were too bright for her or Harry. It must be something for Harvest. The bag crinkled, and Honey froze. Dad sang in the living room and Harvest giggled. Quickly, she pushed the bag aside . . . and came face-to-face with a gross monster.

Big googly eyes rolled. A sharp snout pointed at her beneath a bald green head. It was like a nightmare toy for babies. She couldn't drop it fast enough.

"Honey, did you forget?" her dad called.

She hopped off the dryer. The thing was supposed to be a turtle. She could see it now that she was away from it. But it was deflated. Empty. Probably from one of those stores that helped you stuff it full of fluff. She grabbed the deflated thing and shoved it in the bag, then climbed back up the dryer again. It was as ugly, but with the bright colors and goofy eyes, Harvest would love it. She put the bag back in the cabinet, closed the door, and hurried into the living room with the polka dot PJ's.

Honey tossed her father the pajamas.

"Here you go."

He caught them just before they flew over his head. "Thanks."

"Dad, where is Revered Allen this week? I need to talk to him."

"Really? What is it, Honey? Maybe I can answer your questions."

Honey flopped onto the couch and hugged a pillow. "I'm wondering about the bells. At Old North. Mom said they used to ring."

John pulled up the zipper on Harvest's PJ's. "That's right, they did, didn't they? I'd forgotten."

"Well, I need to talk to Reverend Allen. Mrs. Psalter said we could ring the bells at the Christmas play, but I have to get his permission."

"Reverend Allen is taking a break. That means he can't be bothered." He blew a raspberry into Harvest's neck. "Except for an emergency."

51

"I don't want to bother him. He just needs to say yes or no. Yes, really, and then I won't have to bother him for as long. Isn't that what he's supposed to do? Answer questions and help people? Can't be a Reverend if you don't want people bothering you . . . ."

Her father had stopped wrestling with Harvest and gave Honey a look that spoke volumes. She had crossed the line.

"Fine," she said. She buried her face into the pillow, which oddly enough smelled like root beer. Once Honey settled on a goal, there wasn't much she could think about until she'd accomplished it. And the best way to make progress on a goal was to set a deadline. That's what her life coach told her. Well, she didn't have a life coach, but as soon as she could afford it, she'd hire one. Or be one. But a time limit was set. December 24th. Ringing bells on December 26th wouldn't be the same. She needed to find the Reverend. Now.

"Stop your grumbling," her dad said. "Yep,

I hear you grumbling even if you didn't say anything. Go clean all that yogurt out of your Mom's purse. She's been working hard and could use the break."

Honey tossed the pillow on the couch and dragged herself to the kitchen. She plugged the empty sink, took Mom's purse and turned it upside down. The tissue, gum and receipts clumped together. Even the loose change went splat instead of clink. Honey had to shake the purse hard to get everything to fall out of it — including her mother's wallet. She grabbed a paper towel and picked up the keys to clean them. Her mom's ID from the hospital was next. And the gum . . . well, it tasted pretty good with a coating of yogurt mishmash.

Dad was on the phone ordering pizza when Mom and Harry walked in. Her big brother came to stand by her and looked into the sink.

"Get out of my air," she said. He hadn't done anything to her, but if she didn't bicker, he'd think something was wrong.

53

54

"Not now, Honey," he said.

Something was wrong.

Mom stood in the doorway, waiting for Dad to get off the phone. Her eyes were blotchy. Her nose red. Something was wrong. Harry only shrugged.

Dad finished his call. "What happened to you?"

"I was late picking Harry up, so I had to hurry. And then...."

Harvest walked into the room holding Dad's *Boost 109*.

"You let him drink your energy drink? Are you crazy? Do you know what that'll do? Now we'll be up all night. I've been working day and night — "

"Calm down, Mary," Dad said.

55

But saying *calm down* to mom was like throwing gas on a flame.

"Calm down? Why? Because there's no reason for me to be upset? I shouldn't mind that my two-year-old will be up all night and I'll barely get any sleep before working another shift? I should be happy that I got pulled over for speeding in a school zone . . . after hours . . . and that I didn't have my license because I didn't have my wallet, because my purse is ruined? I should be thrilled!"

Honey stepped closer to Harry. She leaned until her shoulder bumped against him. Mom didn't do so well when she was sleepy. A quick nap and she'd be a new person, but the whole family knew to stay out of her way until then.

"Go," John said. "You're tired. I'll feed the kids."

She nodded and stumbled off. John took the drink from Harvest and ruffled his hair. "I'm the one who needs energy, not you." Harvest grinned, unaware of the trouble he'd caused.

"What did the police say?" Honey asked Harry.

"It happened before she got to me." He looked at the yogurt-coated coins, receipts, and keys in the sink. "Wow. Harvest did that?" He elbowed her. "I guess having three perfect children was too much to ask."

Honey felt warm all over. Her big brother had called her perfect. As much as she pestered Harry, she liked it when he said nice things to her.

58

JAIL HOUSE ROCK

"**A**re we going to the Court House now?" Honey tossed her stained backpack behind the console of the minivan next to Harvest's car seat. "I'll see criminals, won't I? I can ask them what they're in for. I bet they're all guilty...."

"Stop, Honey Moon." Her mother did not look excited. "Your job is to keep a hold of Harvest while I pay my ticket. Do not talk to anyone in there. Do you understand? The people there have broken the law."

"Like you?" Honey asked.

Her mother kept her eyes straight ahead, reached over and cranked up the radio.

60

No one could communicate while Harvest's nursery rhyme CD blared over the speakers. Harvest rocked his car seat while mumbling along. Honey didn't want to talk anyway. She had less than twenty-four hours before the next play practice and she had to muster all her sleuthing skills. She had to find Reverend Allen and get permission to ring the bells. She wanted happy Christmas carols, not dungeon sounds.

They pulled into a parking lot with a bunch of police cruisers and looked for an empty spot. Mary got the last open space. She unbuckled Harvest, gathered her purse, then took a deep breath like she was about to dive off the high-dive.

"Let's go," she said.

They made it inside the courthouse, past the metal detector and the guards before Harvest got fidgety and tried to run away. Honey saw that he had his sights on a large potted plant. The last thing her mom needed was for Harvest to dig in the dirt. Honey took his hand. "Come on, Harvest. Let's sit on the bench. Your mama is doing her best to stay out of jail. She doesn't need you destroying county property."

There was a line of people standing in front of a window with bars. Behind the window, Honey got a glimpse of a woman who looked way too old to be chasing bad guys. A sand-colored bench stretched almost the length of the wall, only leaving room for a square end table full of pamphlets and a dish of butterscotch candy.

Honey lifted Harvest to the bench and got him a piece of candy to pass the time while

61

Mom waited in line. A big teenager came to the back of the line with his dad and stood in front of her. The back of the dad's shirt read Hugo's Repair. The boy's flannel shirt hung halfway tucked in his belt and halfway swinging against his bottom. He never lifted his eyes from his smart phone, even though his dad was talking to him.

"You're lucky it wasn't worse," the dad whispered. "You could've killed someone, driving like that."

Honey scooted Harvest closer against her. A real, live criminal, well sort of criminal, was standing in front of her, although he didn't look so dangerous while texting and getting lectured by his dad.

"How could you live with yourself if that had happened?" the dad said. "Ever think of that?"

"Relax, Dad. Chill," the boy said. His thumbs never stopped tapping on his phone. "Nothing happened. Just a little ticket and some body work. Nothing your boys at the garage can't handle."

His dad's skin turned red above the collar of his rust-colored uniform. He muttered under his breath. "There's no such thing as a little ticket. You don't appreciate how hard I work for this money, and don't get me started on the repairs."

But the boy didn't seem to be impressed. Honey's jaw clenched. How could a boy . . . maybe as much as ten years older than she . . . not take responsibility for his actions? She wanted to grab his phone and stomp on it, but there was a police officer sitting nearby. Stomping phones was probably illegal.

The officer saw her looking at him. He creaked as he left his chair and sat next to her on the bench. All the hardware on his belt jangled against the wooden bench and kept him leaning forward. Was she in trouble?

"May I help you, young lady?"

64

Harvest stared up at him with golf-ball sized eyes. Honey patted his leg and left her hand there for comfort—hers and his.

"No. I don't need anything," Honey nearly whispered. "Just waiting on my mom." Then gathering her courage she asked, "On second thought, I'm wondering how this money thing works. When people break the law, then they have to pay a fine. Is that right?"

The police officer nodded. "Yes, ma'am. Most tickets don't require jail time, just money. Otherwise they wouldn't take the offense seriously."

As this boy wasn't. He was too busy on his phone to notice that his dad had slipped away, leaving him standing in line alone.

Harvest smacked a sticky hand on Honey's knee, but at least he hadn't got her wool skirt or knee socks dirty. She grabbed him another butterscotch and unwrapped the golden wrapper.

65

"I have another question," she said. "What if you were trying to find someone who was hiding out for a little while? What would be the best way to see where they went?"

"First thing we do is run their credit cards and look for their phone signal."

"How do I do that?" she asked.

"You can't. That's police work."

Honey rubbed her chin. Seeing how she probably couldn't get the police to track down the Reverend when he hadn't broken any laws, she'd have to try another way.

"But what if it was a friend?"

"Why wouldn't your friend tell you where she was going?" the officer asked.

"You have no imagination," Honey said.

The officer laughed. "Alright, missy. Let's say your friend left town without telling you. Assuming she's old enough to travel alone, I'd recommend that you get on her computer and see what she's been looking at online. Airlines? Passport information? Hotels?"

Honey frowned. Computer? How on earth could she get to Reverend Allen's computer?

"If you don't have access to her computer, then look for a paper trail. Has she got fliers for resorts? Bills from travel agents? Bids on airfares? Rarely does someone pack up and leave without doing some preparation, and most of the time they leave behind evidence."

"Yes," Honey said. "Evidence." Just what Sherlock always looked for.

The officer smiled.

Reverend Allen's office held the key. Without the Reverend, there'd be no bells. And without the bells, no one would want to come to the Christmas play. And without the Christmas play, Honey would have to go to the Haunted Holiday Festival. If she could just get in the Reverend's office.... The line moved forward again, but new people continued to file in at the back. The boy was nearly to the front of their line when her mother came toward her, putting her wallet in her purse. Her eyebrows rose at seeing Honey's companion.

"I'm sorry, officer Taft. Has she been a problem?" she asked.

The police officer stood. "Not at all. I enjoy helping a fellow detective."

Her mother shot her a questioning look. Honey shrugged as the line of offenders moved forward and the woman behind the glass yelled at the teenager.

"Put that phone away and answer me. What are you here for?"

The young man startled. "I'm Hugo Gillis, Junior. I'm here to pay a ticket."

With a few taps of her keyboard, her eyes narrowed. "What a nice contribution to the county's finances. You're very generous. Pay up."

The boy turned from left to right. Then he spun a complete circle. "Dad? Dad? Where are you?"

"C'mon on, boy. I don't have all day," she said. "Get your wallet out and pay."

"You gotta be kidding me!" he nearly yelled. "I don't have that kind of money. Where's my dad?"

"Your dad's name isn't on this citation. He wasn't the one who broke the law. You are. You don't pay, then you're a wanted man. Might as well turn yourself in now and save us the trouble of hunting you down. Sergeant, could you help over here with this young man?" The woman looked at the officer who had been talking to Honey.

"Let's go, kid." The officer took his arm.

Honey's mother bumped her with her knee. "Do you know anything about this?"

69

Honey could only watch with her mouth hanging open. That phone had been the most important thing in the boy's life a minute ago. Now he would've gladly passed it over to the clerk if he could only see his father again.

"Wait." The clerk's fingers flew over her keyboard. "There's been a mistake. It seems that his fine has already been paid." She looked up in amazement. "Today's your lucky day."

"Are you sure?" the officer said.

"Paid in full. His debt is forgiven." And the clerk didn't look like she believed it.

The officer released his arm. "Wow, kid. I don't know who loved you enough to do that, but you're free. Merry Christmas."

Honey turned to see the boy's father waiting by the door. He hadn't left him after all.

"There's more Christmas here than in the entire Haunted Holiday Festival," Honey said.

Her mother picked up Harvest. "Sometimes, child, you say the most unusual things. Now, let's go home."

HOME RUN

"What are you doing at Claire's house?" Honey dropped her book bag on her bed without lowering her phone and kicked off her shoes. This was the only day of the week they didn't have play practice, and she'd thought Becky would come to her house. It was still early. Just about

A Scary Little Christmas

three o'clock.

"Hanging out. You can come, too."

Honey flopped on her bed. She didn't want to go to Claire's house. She wanted Becky to go with her so they could snoop in Reverend Allen's office. Mrs. Clementine, his secretary, would let Becky in. Everyone trusted Becky. Honey, not so much.

"We've got work to do. Tell Claire you have to go."

"That's not nice. Besides, her big sister Sarah is going to do my makeup. I can't wait."

Honey rolled her eyes. Claire didn't give a flea's life savings for looking pretty, but Becky would love it.

"Listen, Becky. Sarah can do that later. I need your help. We have to find Reverend Allen."

There was a long pause until Becky finally

said, "Ummm, Honey. I don't know if I'm going to be in the play. Miss Fortissimo offered me a solo in the choir's Haunted Holiday performance. I'm going to sing *Have Yourself a Scary Little Christmas*. It's going to be great."

Honey flopped onto her stomach and held herself up by her elbows. "You're going to the Haunted Holiday Festival? For real? Doesn't the word *friendship* mean anything to you? Doesn't the word *commitment* mean anything? How could you do this?" She felt nearly sick to her stomach. Becky knew how important the Christmas pageant was to her. Was this what betrayal felt like?

"Let me ask Claire," Becky said, then the phone went dead. Honey glanced at the screen. Less than a two minute call and she'd lost her temper with her best friend. Or was Becky her best friend anymore? Seemed like all she wanted to do was hang out with Claire.

Her phone buzzed. A text from Becky.

N. Church 5 min omw

83

Honey hopped off the bed, grabbed her shoes and ran into the living room. "I'm going to play practice with Becky," she said.

Her mother looked up for the stack of Christmas cards she was signing. "There's no practice this afternoon."

"We're going to work on something for the play by ourselves," Honey said. Which was true in a way.

"Do you want me to drive you?"

"No thanks." Honey grabbed her coat and hurried out the door. She was on the church grounds before she slowed down. Claire and Becky were waiting for her.

"You're late," Claire said. She tossed a dirty snowball from hand to hand.

Honey was out of breath. "I got here as quick as I could."

"You'd never make it in baseball," Claire said.

"Tagged out on first base every time."

Honey glared. "There are more important things than baseball."

"There are more important things than hearing bells ring," Claire said.

Becky stepped between them. "What do you need us to do, Honey?"

"I thought you wanted to sing at the festival." Honey was trying hard not to sound upset. Especially in front of Claire.

"I do," Becky said. "But I don't want the play to be canceled, either."

"Well, we need to get into Reverend Allen's office to investigate. Then once we figure out where he is, we need to call him about the bells."

"Why don't you just ask where he is?" Claire said.

"Because they won't tell me. And if I ask to go in his office, then they'll know I'm up to something. That's why I need Becky. No one will suspect her."

"Am I going to get in trouble?" Becky chewed on a long brown curl.

Honey shook her head. "You just get us in his office. We aren't going to hurt anything."

Becky tapped her finger on her chin. "I did draw a pretty picture of North Church, well, I copied it from a picture." She dug through her backpack and pulled out a folded piece of card stock. As promised, there was a beautiful picture of the steeple at night surrounded by the Sleepy Hollow town.

"I'll tell Mrs. Clementine I want to hang it in his office to surprise him when he gets back."

"And what am I supposed to do?" Claire asked.

"We don't need you," Honey said. "No one

invited you, anyway."

"But she promised to be in the play." Becky smoothed out the picture. "She's part of the team."

How long before they could make teams again? When was the next election, because Honey didn't remember casting a vote.

"Well, I'm the captain," Honey said. "We'll be back." And she and Becky darted into the side entrance that led to the offices.

11

"Hello, girls." The secretary, a tall woman with red hair put her weight into a giant paper cutter. The handle sliced through the stack of red paper with a bone-chilling whisk. "How can I help you?"

Becky held up her picture. "I made this for Reverend Allen and I want to hang it in his office. When he gets back he'll be so surprised! He loves my drawings."

The secretary moved the paper around for

the next cut. "Just leave it on my desk and I'll put it in there."

Becky blinked her big, brown eyes. Honey was impressed. She could never fake that level of hurt and innocence. "But I want it to be special. I want to hang it right behind his computer."

"And that's where I'll put it. He'll see it first thing. Good bye, girls."

She left no room for arguing. Becky dragged her feet to the door. The secretary paused, looking straight at Honey through her glasses which had slipped down her pointy nose. She didn't even blink until Honey had reached the door.

Fail. Big, fat fail.

"Whaddya find out?" Claire tossed the snowball up and caught it with her bare hand.

"Nothing," Honey said. "She didn't let us in."

"What kind of church is this?" Claire asked.

"One that doesn't give children unlimited access to the pastor's study," Honey said.

"Now that you mention it," Becky replied, "I guess I can't blame her. It is the Reverend's private office."

"You know, this snowball is more ice than snow." Claire squeezed it hard. "It'd raise a welt if I threw it at you."

"Then let's not do that." On the best of days, Honey wasn't the most patient person. Today of all days, she shouldn't have to deal with Claire.

"That window there." Claire pointed. "Is that the pastor's office?"

"What of it?" Honey asked. "I'm sure it's locked, too."

"Be right back." Claire dashed off to the garden shed in the corner of the courtyard and returned with a snow shovel. "You want in that office?"

Honey's pulse picked up. She looked at the shovel, then at the girl with the baseball cap. There were times you knew you were making a deal with the devil, but in this case, she was making a deal to save Christmas, which wasn't the same thing.

"What are you going to...?"

Claire tossed the snowball straight up in the cold air, swung the shovel like a baseball bat, and BAM! hit it with the shovel like she was an All-Star slugger. The ball of ice flew like a comet directly toward the church office. Straight as an arrow to the window.

"Noooo...!" hollered Honey. But it was too late. It hit with a smack. Glass shattered. Shards mixed with the dirty snow melting on the ground beneath.

Claire tapped the shovel against the sole of her tennis shoe. "You can thank me later."

ON A MISSIOIN

The damage was done. No use crying over spilt milk, or in this case, broken glass. Plans formed and re-formed as Honey tried to figure out how to best use this to their advantage. But she had to think fast. It wouldn't be long before Mrs. Clementine came outside to look for the culprit.

The door flew opened. "What just

happened?" The secretary stepped. outside holding her sweater tightly around her shoulders. She turned to look at the church. Her mouth dropped open. "Did you do this?"

Claire removed her cap. "It's my fault. I'm sorry. Let me help you clean it up."

Becky knelt in the snow and gingerly picked up a piece of glass. "Do you have a trash bin out here?"

Honey raced to the door. "I'll clean the office."

Not waiting for the secretary to stop her, she ran into the building, darted past the secretary's desk, and ran down the short hall to the Reverend's office. Once there she had a moment of misgiving. The only time she'd even been in Reverend Allen's office was with her parents. They'd visited a lot when all that strange stuff started happening to Harry. I mean, what would you do if your son suddenly could do magic...real magic? Wouldn't you want to talk to someone that was in good with God?

And every time they visited it was a serious occasion — be on your best behavior, no gum, Dad sits up straight in the chair and all that good stuff.

What would her parents think of her going inside without Reverend Allen's permission? If that were a test question, Honey knew the answer, but sacrifices had to be made.

"Sorry, Rev," she whispered as she eased the door open. Besides the light from the recently opened window, it was dark. Heavy shadows stretched from a hall tree across the bookcases. No light came from the computer screen. Not eerie, really. More weighty. Like the room was watching her, but only for her own good.

Honey walked behind the desk. She'd never been on this side of it before. She looked at the two chairs where her family had sat to talk about Harry. They'd pulled up the chair from the corner, and she'd stood behind her dad. From the pastor's view, the room didn't look nearly as intimidating. The clock was cleverly placed on the opposite wall so he could keep on schedule without them knowing he was checking the time. Smart man. And she had to find him.

The desk was clean. Only a block of sticky notes, and an old-fashioned phone with a lot of buttons and a cord. Behind the desk, against the wall, sat the computer and her best chance at finding the Reverend. Fliers, mail, and jotted notes littered this area, and even a row of Hot Wheels cars. That made her pause. The learned Reverend collected toy cars? Hmmm. But just as quickly she got back to business and flipped through the paper. Pages of notes scribbled on legal pads, lists of people and hospital names, a thank-you card from a church member — lots of correspondence, but nothing about a vacation.

Honey couldn't help but feel guilty, but she kept telling herself she was doing good. To turn people away from the festival and toward a normal Christmas celebration would be a good thing.

Footsteps sounded in the hall. Honey spun in the spinning chair and grabbed the trashcan out from beneath the desk. Holding it in one hand, she threw herself on the floor and managed to get a few pieces of glass in the trashcan before Mrs. Clementine came to the door.

"Just get the big pieces," she said. "I'll vacuum up the rest."

"Are you going to call him?" Honey asked. "Doesn't he need to know about his office window being broken?"

"We're not to interrupt him unless it's an emergency," she said. "Do you think a broken window is an emergency? After the potluck salmonella poisoning, I can assure you this is not an emergency."

Honey picked up the melting snowball and tossed it out the window.

"Hey," Claire yelled from outside. "Be careful. You might hit something."

Now she was worried?

The secretary inspected the window frame. Shards of glass hung in the frame like the jagged shark teeth. "I'll get the maintenance man to fix it. He'll patch it up until we can get the glass company out." She turned to Honey. "And I'm afraid I will have to call your parents. It might be an accident, but word will get out. Better for them to have heard it from me."

Which was debatable, but Honey wouldn't argue. She reached over the trashcan to drop more glass in when a picture caught her eye. There among the Tootsie Roll wrappers was a brochure featuring a couple on a porch overlooking the ocean.

Cape Sanctuary Bed & Breakfast - Because Life Was Meant to be Appreciated

Honey caught a hold of the corner of the brochure and shook off the glass. She flipped it over to the back. The phone number was circled.

BINGO!

Thank you, Officer Taft.

Mrs. Clementine was saying something about her cutting herself and getting an infection, but Honey didn't care. She'd found what she was looking for. It was time to go. She nodded in agreement and slipped the card beneath the trashcan. Then using it to shield her treasure, she carried the can back to its place under the desk. By the time she stood up again, the travel brochure was safely in her pocket.

"Sorry again about the window," Honey said on her way outside as she rushed to huddle with the girls.

They ran a safe distance from the church into the town green past the tent. Becky dusted the snow off a bench and they sat together.

"Mission accomplished," Honey said. "I found him." She produced the brochure and pointed to the number. "All we got to do is call him. He'll say we can ring the bells, and then they'll have to keep the Christmas play going."

"Do you think the bells will make that much of a difference?" Becky tucked her hands inside her pockets and shivered.

Somehow this was already about more than hearing some bells. It was about the way Miss Fortissimo had so easily dismissed their Christmas play. *Oh, you have a play? That's too bad because the Haunted Holiday Festival is going to be even better.* It was about the way that all the shiny, golden warmth of Christmas had turned into cold, dull, metal in Sleepy Hollow. Instead of a Christmas tree on the town square, there was a Headless Horseman covered in orange lights. Instead of cheerful yard decorations, there were scary angels and creepy snowmen. Blood-thirsty, dark songs taking the place of peace-on-Earth-goodwill-to-men. Not that the scary wasn't funny sometimes, but she couldn't find the true Christmas love in Sleepy Hollow anywhere.

Honey shrugged. "We won't know until we try." She took out her phone and punched the numbers.

"Hello, this is Honey Moon. I'm looking for Reverend.... No, I don't need to book my Honey Moon. I'm only ten. My name is Honey. Honey Moon. Is the Reverend . . . ? Yes, my parents are so clever. Have you thought about what I live with?" At least she didn't have to tell them that her brothers were named Harry and Harvest. "What I need is to talk to Reverend Allen. Is he available?"

What followed was some hem-hawing about as the woman explained that she wasn't supposed to disturb Mr. Allen, but soon a very familiar voice came over the line. Honey could hardly believe it. Butterflies congregated in her stomach.

"Honey Moon, how did you get my number?"

"Hello, Reverend. I have an important question about the Christmas Eve service."

She pulled herself up to her full height. "You see, I'm helping Mrs. Psalter work out the details for the Christmas Eve play and we were wondering — "

"I'm on a Sabbatical to prepare for the new year. Mrs. Clementine was not to give this number to anyone."

"And I won't give it to anyone, either. Well, no one besides Becky and Claire. You don't know Claire. She doesn't go to church and she spits like a boy and loves baseball more than anything. Any, boy, can she hit. But what we were wondering was if we could ring the bells for the Christmas Eve play. You know, how they used to?" Honey tapped the phone onto speaker so Becky and Claire could hear.

There was a long pause. Finally he spoke again. "Of course you can ring bells, shake tambourines, toot a flute. Whatever Mrs. Psalter decides."

"No, I mean the big bells in the steeple. Those are the bells we want to ring."

He took a deep breath. "I see. While I appreciate your enthusiasm, as well as your ingenuity in finding my phone number, ringing those bells is impossible. That belfry is over four hundred years old. The boards are rotten, the stairs are rickety. It's not safe to go up there. We can't be responsible for what happens. Get some jingle bells if you'd like, but the church bells have to stay silent. They're just not safe."

91

TO TUTOR SCOOTER

Honey clicked off her phone and stared at the blank screen. "I can't believe it. How can he say no? How can he want them to stay quiet?"

Becky craned her head back and followed the lines of the steeple up. "I'm glad we called him. We could get hurt going up there.

Can you imagine if those bells crashed to the ground? That would be a total disaster."

"I'm not afraid," Claire said. "I'd still do it."

Honey studied the tall structure. She was afraid. Couldn't even pretend that she wasn't, but she'd go anyway. She'd go because she was afraid, but she was more afraid of having the Haunted Holiday Festival be the only Christmas celebration in Sleepy Hollow.

94

"I've got a plan," she said. She dropped her phone into her book bag and studied the steeple. The glass windows reflected the late afternoon light back at her. It was impossible to see inside them. Were they painted or boarded up? It didn't matter. She'd know soon enough.

"We have practice tomorrow night," Honey said. "That's when we're going in the belfry."

"Awesome!" said Claire.

"We can't," said Becky. "Mrs. Psalter will never let us."

"We aren't going to ask," said Honey. The final details were falling into place even as she spoke. "After practice we sneak away from everyone else and we hide. We wait until Mrs. Psalter leaves and then we climb up into the belfry. If we each bring a flashlight . . . ."

"Wait," said Claire. "Won't our mothers be waiting on us after practice? They'll come looking for us."

"Let's use your sister," Honey said. Claire's big sister Sarah used to babysit the Moon children. Now, with Harry being thirteen, they were allowed to be home by themselves for short periods of time, unless mother was working all day and then Harvest's nanny stayed. "Let's have Sarah pick us up. We'll tell her that we're staying afterwards to practice something. She won't come until later and we'll have time to check it out."

Becky chewed on an already nubby fingernail. Claire swung one arm around as if practicing for fast-pitch softball. She pretend lobbed a ball directly at one of the port-apotties that had been set up along the street for the big event. The girls also saw generators, and picnic tables being set up along with vendor booths and craft displays. It looked like fun if it weren't for the terrifying decorations.

"I'll ask her," Claire said. "I'll tell her to pick us up thirty minutes after practice. That should give us time."

"But what are we hoping to find?" Becky asked. "If it's too dangerous...."

"What if it's not as dangerous as he thinks?" asked Honey. "Or what if it's easy to fix? Why couldn't the church get a carpenter to fix the stairs? But we need to know first. Then we can ask for help."

"In the meantime," said Claire, "I'm working on my Haunted Holiday costume. I'm going to be a melting Frosty the snowman. Mom is making me a skinny snowman suit with bones sticking out and it'll leak water everywhere as I go. I'm going to cry, *I'm melting, I'm melting,* just like the witch in *The Wizard of Oz.*"

Honey tucked her escaping shirttails into her pleated skirt. And she'd thought the shepherd costume was bad.

"As long as you both think it's safe . . . ," Becky said. "I think Mom will let Sarah bring me home. She likes your sister."

Everyone liked Sarah. Especially Harry. He was in love with her. But he was thirteen and Sarah was sixteen. Three years was way too big of a difference. Honey frowned. Then again, Scooter was thirteen and she was ten. Somehow that didn't seem as bad.

Scooter!

"I'm supposed to be at Mrs. Psalter's tonight!" Honey jumped from the bench. Her saddle shoes hit the ground. "I forgot I have to help Scooter."

Honey ran all the way to the Psalters' house. By the time she arrived, her sock had bunched up inside her shoe and she was sweaty beneath her coat. After ringing the doorbell she bent to tug on her sock, but the wrinkle wouldn't leave. Mrs. Psalter answered the door.

Honey could not contain her enthusiasm. "I spoke to Reverend Allen."

"You did?" Mrs. Psalter said. "But how—"

"Don't worry about it," Honey said. "The important thing is that we're working on the bells."

"Honey Moon," Mrs. Psalter said, "you are a caution."

Honey smiled, mostly on the inside. "Oh, let's just say I'm good at writing essays AND at sleuthing."

Mrs. Psalter led Honey to a dining room table covered in costumes. She lifted a quilted sewing box off and pushed the costumes to the side. "Scooter, Honey is here. Bring your essay."

Honey took a seat in the fancy, high-backed chair. Would he really hate her forever? She thought of his mean comments during practice and braced for the worst.

Scooter strutted down the stairs and into the dining room. His athletic pants swished with each step. His dark hair dripped and he smelled good. Must have just got out of the shower after basketball practice.

Harry had such cool friends.

99

"Here's my paper." He shoved three crumpled pages toward her and moved the next chair as far away as he could. "I didn't have much time to work on it. I'm going to do it better before I turn it in and all, but I've been busy lifting weights and shooting baskets." His eyes never left the table.

Honey picked up the paper. When Scooter was at her house hanging out with Harry, he always ignored her. Now he had to pay attention, but she hadn't thought about ex-actly what she was going to say to him. What if his paper was awful? She didn't want to make him feel stupid.

She scanned over it. Couldn't concentrate. Tried again. What was it even about?

"Stop breathing," she said. "I can't focus."

"Tell me when you're done." And he got up and went into the kitchen.

Honey gripped the paper. From the kitchen she recognized the familiar voice of his mother arguing with her son.

Scooter said, "She told me to leave. She's

grading it now... She's not thirsty. She just got here."

Honey licked her lips. Actually she was thirsty, but that would have to wait. The paper was a compare and contrast. That was easy enough. And his topic was ninjas versus gladiators. Honey settled in as she read. Besides covering a boring topic, it wasn't that bad. Just needed some work on the structure. Scooter stepped into the room with a sneer on his face and two Cokes in hand.

"Here. Mom said you are thirsty."

Honey didn't even touch the can. Instead she held out the paper. "This is good," she said. "You did a good job in the introduction telling why ninjas and gladiators were both epic warriors."

"I did?" He sat. "Well, it is important. Gotta give respect where it's due."

"And you give a lot of descriptions about what makes their different fighting styles unique, but what would make the paper move from a C to an A would be the structure of the paper."

Scooter grabbed a pen and a blank piece of paper from his folder. "What do you mean?"

He was listening to her. Scooter Psalter was treating her like she was thirteen. Or at least twelve.

"In the paragraphs following the intro, describe how ninjas and gladiators are alike — training, fighting with swords, taking on more than one enemy at a time. Don't talk about any differences yet. Then once you've written about everything you can think of, then start over with ways they are different."

He took the paper. "I thought I did both in here, already."

"But keep them separate," she said. "Compare first, how they are the same, and once you've done that, then contrast. You have that in here, but it's mashed together like yogurt."

"What?" Scooter said.

"Never mind," Honey said.

Scooter's pen moved on the blank page. "That should be easy enough," he said. "I can cut and paste this, then read through . . . ."

From the other room they could hear the front door opening. Scooter ticked off sentences from his first draft. "Thanks, Honey. I didn't know what to expect."

103

"Scooter? What's going on here? What are you doing?"

Honey looked up. It was her brother, Harry. He made a face like he'd just caught a whiff of Harvest's dirty diaper.

Scooter grabbed his papers and shoved them into his book bag. "Finally! I'm tired of babysitting your bratty sister. Take her home."

Honey couldn't stop blinking. Harry couldn't stop laughing.

"Mom told me she was here working on homework with you, but I didn't believe her. The day Honey needs help from you on home-work—well, I know she's faking it. She probably asked for help just because she thinks you're C-U-T-E."

Honey jumped to her feet. "Shut up, Harry! I did not ask for help. I...I...." There was Scooter looking like he'd just swallowed a worm and it was crawling back up his throat. She couldn't tell Harry that Scooter needed her help. He'd bug Scooter about it forever. She crossed her arms and stomped her foot. "I'm going home. And if you tell anyone, I'll make sure everyone knows you sleep with that stuffed rabbit."

She grabbed her coat and book bag and stomped out of the house. She would never speak to Harry again. Harry would get the silent treatment for the rest of the week.

Harry ran down the street after her. "Leave my friends alone," he said. "It's creepy for you to go to their house. He won't hang out with me anymore if you keep this up."

"Shut up," she said. "You don't know anything."

"I know when my little sister is stepping on my turf. What would you say if you went to Becky's and found Harvest there playing blocks with her? Wouldn't you be mad?"

Harvest would be better than Claire. Honey already felt like she was losing her friend.

"You're so busy with all your magic shows and appearances you don't have time for your friends anyway."

"That's not true. Scooter, Declan, and Hao all hang out with me. We're the Good Mischief club. I include them."

But he didn't include her. And sometimes it hurt.

106

A MOST
DANGEROUS QUEST

"Are they gone yet?" Becky's muffled voice sounded from beneath a table while Claire lay on her side, her knees pulled in like she was a pill bug. Play practice had just ended and the girls were waiting for everyone to leave.

Honey peeked out the window. "Mrs. Psalter is still in the parking lot. Don't turn on any flashlights yet." Her heart raced a little because she was thinking that maybe, just maybe she should be worried about the bells. What if Reverend Allen had all the right info? She looked back at her friends and yes, she mostly considered Claire to be her friend. She just wasn't sure she was ready to share Becky with her. But there they all were, planning together to ring the bells. Now that's something only true friends plan to do together. Claire was going to wear a melty Frosty the Snowman costume for Halloween but maybe it was really Honey who was doing some melting. Her heart, anyway. She heard a car door slam and lifted her nose above the window sill. The lot was empty.

"Everyone is gone," Honey called. "Let's go."

Switching their flashlights on, the girls crawled out of hiding and hurried to the big arch at the front of North Church. Several white paneled doors lined the room. One went to the basement, one to the coat closet, but there was one that they had never seen opened. There was a sign on it that read: NOT AN EXIT.

Honey twisted the brass door knob. It clattered as it rotated round and round uselessly. "It's broken."

Claire traced the door with her beam of light. "Up there. Those nails are bent to hold the door closed."

"I know what to get." Becky dashed off, her flashlight beam bouncing.

Maybe having Claire around wasn't so bad. Honey wouldn't have wanted to wait by herself. She hated being alone, especially with the wicked statues visible from the Haunted Holiday in the next lot.

"This is a blast," Claire said. "I've never broke into a building before."

Were they criminals? Was Honey the ringleader?"

"We have to try and save the season," she explained, making the excuse to herself as much as to Claire. "It's a good cause."

In a few minutes Becky returned with a butter knife from the kitchen. Becky tried to reach the nails but even standing on her tiptoes she couldn't reach.

"No problem," Honey said looking at Claire. "You can get on your hands and knees and be like a step stool."

"Me? Why not you?"

"Cause I'm the leader."

"Ugh," But Claire bent down and let Becky stand on her back anyway. "Hurry," Claire said. "You're heavy."

Becky used the knife to pry a nail and slowly straighten it. Another nail. And another nail and . . . "

"Finish!" cried Claire. "I'm going to fall!"

Becky pried the last nail and jumped from Claire's back just in time because Claire went SPLAT on the floor like a belly-flopper.

"Sorry," Becky said.

But Honey was already pulling the door open. Cobwebs covered the opening. A few bulletins littered the floor, the top one from a 1994 service. Becky took the knife, punctured the web and dragged it out down.

"Ewww...," Honey said.

"They're just spiders." Becky swung the tongs around, but the sticky web wouldn't fall.

Claire shone the light on the ancient stairs disappearing up into the dark, narrow opening. "Let's do this."

"Ready?" Honey said.

"Ready," Claire and Becky said.

Honey stepped on the first step. It felt only

111

a little rickety under her foot. "I think we should go one at a time," she said. "The steps might not hold all of us at the same time."

"Good thinking," Becky said.

Honey climbed the stairs like she was walking over glass, trying to stay on her toes. She shone the light up and was finally able to see the bell-ringing room. The old, dusty smell made her nose itch. She coughed and sneezed once so loudly all three girls held their breath in case of an avalanche.

Honey reached the top and stumbled once as her toe got caught in a knothole. "It's okay," she called. "I'm safe. Come on up."

Becky and Claire followed and soon they were all standing in the belfry. They shone their lights around at the long, thick and heavy ropes used to pull the bells.

"Wow," Becky said. "I can't believe it. We are probably the first people inside here in years.

The beams of their flashlights followed the ropes up to a crude, wooden ceiling built of thick boards. The holes sawn in the ceiling were rough, but each had a hole with a rope through it. Twelve holes. Twelve ropes. One for each bell-ringer.

And there were windows, too. Actually the windows were more like openings in the brick tower. The girls looked down and out on the sparkling town of Sleepy Hollow, so quaint from the distance. No sign at all that the decorations were frightening instead of joyful. Even the grotesque Headless Horseman statue looked like another brave Civil War general. Just a peaceful, snowy village. Her parents and brothers were down there some-where, watching TV, doing homework, cleaning up from supper—never knowing that some-one that loved them was looking down on them at that moment.

"One of us has to get up there and check out the swing things," Honey said.

"I'll go," Claire said.

113

Honey took a breath and shook her head. "No. I'm the leader."

"Do you want us to wait for you here?" Becky asked, slinging her flashlight beam in Honey's direction, but she only succeeded in awakening something vile. A black varmint swooped down toward them, darting between their heads with wicked precision, then swung around and sped through them again on its way up.

114

The banister pressed into Honey's back as she tried to become one with the white paint on the walls. Claire was still ducking with her hands over her head, and Becky looked like she might faint.

"Was that a bat?" Becky gasped. "I can't believe I'm doing this."

Claire recovered quickly, caught one of the ropes and leaned her weight against it. "Shouldn't we give it try?"

"No!" Honey said. "If anyone hears them ringing, we're in trouble."

"Trouble, smouble. We succeeded. We proved that it isn't dangerous up here. We'll let the bells ring for Christmas Eve."

"Getting caught inside the church wasn't part of the deal," Becky said. "Let's go home, and then next practice we can show Mrs. Psalter...."

But Claire wasn't waiting. She grabbed onto one of the ropes and pulled—just a little at first. "Listen," she said. "Listen for the bell."

Nothing.

Silence.

Claire pulled harder.

But nothing.

"You did it too slow," Becky said. "You have to get the bell swinging faster."

"I'll try another one," Claire said. She walked over to the next rope, but Honey wasn't

115

interested. Already a dread fear was filling her heart. Something wasn't right. Something was hidden. A plain wooden ladder made of ancient planks was nailed into the wall. It went up until it dead-ended at a trap door. She tucked her flashlight under her chin like she had seen her father do. She began climbing the ladder as fast as she could. She had to see the bells for herself. At the top, she put her head against the trapdoor and strained upward. It gave an inch at a time, raining dust and debris with every move. Finally it reached the tipping point and crashed open, clearing the way.

Honey climbed up the last rungs and studied the belfry in the moonlight.

It was empty.

No bells. Just the huge structures of wood beams and wheels. The twelve bronze bells were missing.

"THEY'RE GONE!" Honey called down to Becky and Claire. "The bells are gone."

"Impossible! Maybe they are further up," Becky said.

"There isn't any more up!" Honey shouted. "Someone has stolen the bells."

No bells. No ringing. Nothing. She wouldn't ever hear them pealing across the hills and valleys like her mom remembered. Honey felt empty. The disappointment was more than missing out on something cool. It was almost like she missed seeing someone. Like being invited to a birthday party, but the birthday kid doesn't show up. That's what it felt like. An awful practical joke.

Honey climbed back down the ladder. "I can't believe it!"

Becky took her hand. "I'm sorry, Honey. I know you were counting on ringing them for the Christmas Eve service."

Claire dusted her hands. "I didn't expect this, but at least we have the Festival. It's going to be great."

127

Just great.

Honey looked around the room one last time, because she still couldn't believe her eyes. How had they just disappeared? Bells that big, that heavy, couldn't be carried out in secret. Someone had to know something.

"We'd better go," Claire said. "Sarah will get suspicious if we wait too long."

But Honey was already suspicious. She had to get to the bottom of this.

"I'm calling the Reverend." Honey led the way down the stairs, no longer afraid of some spider webs and bats. They'd better be afraid of her, because she was on a mission. They gathered their bags, exited through the self-locking doors, and by the time they were in Sarah's truck, Honey was scrolling for the phone number to the *Cape Sanctuary Bed & Breakfast*.

Becky nudged Honey's shoulder and gestured toward Sarah. They hadn't told Sarah the truth about the bells.

Honey sucked all the air out of the truck cabin and said, "Look Sarah. We did something after practice but you have to promise not to tell a single living soul."

Sarah pulled the truck along a curb on Mt. Sinai Road. "What? What did you girls do?"

Honey swallowed and then told her the whole story.

"So you see," Honey said. "We just wanted to ring the bells for Christmas to remind Sleepy Hollow that every day doesn't have to be Halloween."

Sarah shook her head. "You could have been killed."

"But we weren't," Becky said.

Honey tapped her phone. "I'm calling Reverend Allen right now."

Sarah shook her head. "Great. Now I'm an accessory to your crimes."

"It's Honey again," Honey said into her phone. "Yeah, sorry to bother you, but since you were so worried about the belfry being dangerous I thought you'd like to know that the stairs are fine, because me, Becky and Claire went up them, after practice, but Mrs. Psalter doesn't know. Please don't tell her, because we waited until she was gone. Anyway, the reason I'm calling is because I went up there to see if we could ring the bells, but the bells are gone!" Honey needed another deep breath before she could continue.

"Hello? Are you there?" Honey asked. "I couldn't hear you, but the bells are gone. There aren't any bells up there. We tried ringing them and nothing happened, so I went higher, and it's empty. The bells are nowhere. Did you know that? Do you know what happened to them?"

Here Honey waited while he sputtered. Reverend Allen said something about forgetting and then something else about it happening before he came to Sleepy Hollow. He didn't remember exactly, but it seemed like he heard that the city had something to do with the remodeling of the steeple. They'd helped the church out. The Selectmen would know.

"What's going on?" Sarah whispered. "Are you in trouble?"

Claire propped her feet on the dash of Sarah's truck. "The church is in trouble. If someone can carry those bells out of the church without them knowing, next thing you know they'll be missing their pipe organ."

131

"Someone knows where they went," Honey said to the Reverend, "and we're going to help you find them. Alright, then. Good-night and sorry to call you again. See you on Christmas Eve."

She clicked off her phone.

"What did he say?" Sarah asked. Sarah might be Claire's big sister, but Honey still liked her. Not as much as Harry did, but that was a different story. "Did the city take them?"

"Something like that," Honey said. "Maybe we should talk to the Selectmen—"

"I'll tell you this," said Sarah. "You won't learn anything by talking to the mayor or the Selectmen. They have more secrets than Miss Fortissimo's diary. Harry says some of what the Selectmen know is pretty dark. You need to do your own investigation. Find out when the North Church was remodeled or if there was repair work done. See who was in charge then. Do your homework." Sarah was on the school paper at the high school. She was the one who discovered the shrinking pudding portions in the cafeteria's lunches and started a petition. She was legit.

And Honey knew exactly where to go to dig up dirt.

The library.

MELTED

The last day of school before the winter break had been filled with practice and planning for the ultimate adventure — the Haunted Holiday Festival. With every description of the costumes, pranks and frights, Honey's mood got darker and darker. Without the bells, they might as well cancel the play. Without the play, Honey would have to spend Christmas Eve in the new pit of despair constructed by the city of Sleepy Hollow, her dreams of a normal Christmas fading like a poinsettia in January.

Tonight, the girls only had an hour before practice started, so they had to hurry. They ran to the library as soon as school ended. Clomping in their snow boots through the gritty sidewalks, they splashed and laughed along the way. They were honing in. Could smell blood. Soon they'd find the culprit.

Honey went first to Elvira Scudwell, the librarian. The three girls leaned their tummies against the circulation desk as she peered over the rims of her glasses at them.

"How can I help you?" The skin on her hands looked as brittle as the yellow pages she was flipping through.

"We're looking for some Sleepy Hollow history," Honey said. "Trying to learn something about our town."

The woman leaned back with a smile. "Oh, good. I was afraid you wanted Christmas werewolf books. I declare if I never see another frightful Christmas book, it won't be too soon." She walked from behind the counter and they followed her to the archives. "Do you know the dates you're looking for? We've had some problem with our old newspaper. Seems like they were printed with bad ink. It keeps disappearing, like someone doesn't want anyone to remember what's happened here."

The girls exchanged glances. "Weird," Claire said.

"We don't know the exact date," Honey said, "but we want to know what happened to the church bells."

Mrs. Scudwell removed her glasses. "The church bells? That's a good question. I haven't heard them for a long time." She paused and a dreamy look came over her. "Gosh, they were pretty. I remember when I was your age . . ."

Honey cleared her throat.

"Oh, right," Mrs. Scudwell said. "That was just before Sleepy Hollow officially became what it is today. Sad to see all of our holidays disappear into one extended Halloween, but it has been good for business, or so they say." She went to a shelf of narrow slots, and ran her finger down the stack. "Here we go. This is about the time they did the remodel on the North Church."

126

She removed the large, flat box and laid it on the table. Honey's nose itched. Becky sneezed. Claire looked bored. Mrs. Scudwell opened the box to show a stack of newspapers lying as flat as if they'd been ironed.

"Can I trust you girls?"

Honey nodded. "I do research in here all the time. I'll be careful."

The librarian fixed Claire with a skeptical eye. "I heard that some young lady broke a window at the church yesterday. Wouldn't want that kind of accident here."

Claire turned the brim of her baseball cap backwards and kept her chin ducked, but as soon as librarian left she bounded back to her old self.

Honey carefully turned the old newspaper pages.

"See anything?" Claire asked.

"Hold your horses," Honey said. She scanned the first page and found nothing about the church. Scanning was easy because, just as librarian said, there were whole sections of the paper that had faded. No words. Honey dearly hoped that somewhere those records existed. If someone could change history, they could change the future. Quickly she made it through the first few editions of the paper. Then on the fifth page of a February issue, she saw something.

"Church remodel underway," she read aloud. "Kligore Construction has been hired to repair the worn and dangerous staircase of the North Church bell tower."

"It didn't look repaired to me," said Claire. "That staircase was ancient."

"Does it say anything about them removing the bells?" asked Becky.

Honey scanned. "Yes. It says the floor of the ringing chamber will be replaced and the staircases reinforced with new timber. Oh and the bells will be removed, then returned after everything has been replaced."

"But nothing was fixed," said Claire. "They took the bells and didn't fix anything."

The rest of the article had faded into oblivion. Honey turned the page, wondering at all the important information that had been lost, or hidden. Surely there was a clue somewhere.

"So that's when it went up?" Becky pointed at a picture of the famous Headless Horseman statue on the square. The black and white photo was grainy, but the image was unmistakable. Atop the granite pedestal stood the bronze statue. It wasn't finished, but its grasping hands already held the sneering jack-o-lantern. "I always wondered whose decision it was to build it."

"It says here that the Selectmen voted to designate a spot on the city green to the statue, and the statue itself was donated by Kligore Construction." Honey kept her finger on the caption. "Donated by Kligore Construction? The bronze statue was donated by Kligore Construction? The same people who took the bells out of the church?"

"And didn't return them?" Claire's eyes blazed. "Of all the crummy, dirty tricks."

"I don't get it," said Becky. "Why?"

"Don't you see," Honey said. "They used the metal from the bells to make the Headless Horseman statue." Honey felt her knees shake. There were no bells left. The beautiful music had been destroyed for an ugly, hateful statue of a decapitated horseman. How had

129

this stayed a secret? Didn't anyone care?

"Those Selectmen, I'd like to ring their bells." Claire's anger was almost comforting.

Becky looked at her watch. "We have to hurry. We're going to be late to practice."

They gently boxed the old newspapers and left. Honey didn't look right or left, just stayed between Becky and Claire as they hurried to practice. The spooky, colored lights from the storefronts lit their way, until they turned down the darker streets of the neighborhoods and finally at North Church.

But cars were pulling out of the parking lot.

"Did we miss practice?" Becky asked. "We're not late."

Mrs. Psalter was standing on the steps talking to Brianna's mother, Mrs. Royal. Brianna's angel costume had been decorated with even more pieces of tinfoil and jewels since last time. It was a mess, and so was she. Her eyes watered and her nose was red. When she saw the girls coming, she turned her face away.

"There you are, girls," said Mrs. Psalter. "I sent word to your parents, but you weren't home. We've cancelled the Christmas Eve program. Reverend Allen told me there was no chance of doing a bell-ringing. And besides, the school choir is performing across the street at the Haunted Holiday Festival at the same time. We've had too many kids drop out." She looked sad and disappointed. "Can't beat Halloween."

131

"I don't quit," Honey said. Brianna lifted her head suddenly. Honey continued. "I'll be a shepherd and angel both. I can learn the lines. The four of us will do the whole thing."

"Maybe next year," Mrs. Psalter said. "This year, let's just go and enjoy the festival. It's what everyone wants to do, evidently."

Claire clapped a hand on Honey's back. "Sorry it didn't work out for you, but life ain't fair. Why don't you come to the festival with me? We can put together a gross costume for you. I've got it! Mrs. Claus the Vampire Slayer. That could be you."

Becky giggled. "C'mon, Honey. Say you'll do it. You'll get bonus points in choir."

"I don't know. I can't decide right now." Honey dug her toe in the snow. "I'll let you know tomorrow."

132

"Okay," Becky said. "Let's go home."

They walked around the park, past the twisted, winter wonderland. Lights shone and twinkled as the workers made the last minute adjustments. Fires crackled in large metal drums with the name Kligore imprinted on them. Honey grimaced.

"Look at the gingerbread house," Becky cried. "When did that go up?"

The life-sized gingerbread house was covered in candy and icing with a white stone walkway lined with giant lollipops on either side. It didn't look scary at all. Honey felt a little better. A gingerbread house. That was fun, cheerful and Christmassy. Maybe she could find something that didn't scream Halloween.

"It's real candy," Claire said. She poked at a gumdrop on the wall and motioned to a woman on a ladder who was gluing graham cracker shingles on the roof with icing. "Can I eat this?"

The woman's eyes gleamed. "Tomorrow you can. I'll be all ready for the little boys and girls tomorrow. Bring your friends."

"We can't wait!" Becky clapped her hands. Then turned to Honey and said, "See, it's not all scary. See you tomorrow."

Honey started out on the long walk home. Discovering the bells had been melted down was the worst thing that had happened all year. She'd now have to try and make the best of the holiday. She still had her Christmas present to open on Christmas Eve. She'd finally have her gown and that was going to be splendiferous. Or so she thought.

FOR SUCH A TIME AS THIS

"I don't want to be Mrs. Claus Vampire Slayer," Honey said over the phone. "Claire's crazy."

"Dress up pretty, then," Becky suggested. "Have you got your yellow dress, yet? You could wear it and be the Star of Christmas."

Honey stopped chewing the end of her braid. Would she have time to get dressed up after they opened their gifts? She wrapped the braid around her finger, hoping for some curl. Maybe mom would even let her wear lip-gloss. And maybe Scooter would see her.

"Maybe Scooter will see you," Becky said, reading her mind like only a best friend can do.

"Gross!" Honey said. "That's disgusting." But she looked in the mirror all the same, wondering what the dress looked like and if it was warm enough to wear without her coat. "I'll call you if I decide to come," she said finally. "But I'm not singing in the school choir. Miss Fortissimo isn't getting her Christmas wish."

"Honey," her mother called. "Are you ready for presents?"

"Gotta go!" Honey hung up and skipped into the living room. The Moons always went full tilt on the decorations. They had a large, Douglas fir tree decorated with natural and glass ornaments. Honey's favorite was the red glass heart. It was very delicate, paper-thin glass that allowed the twinkling lights on the tree to shine through. A large wreath made of pinecones with a huge, green ribbon hung over the mantle. The nativity scene was on the oak mantle, minus one astronaut shepherd who was still in orbit. Pine roping stretched all around the room with tiny white lights wrapped around the evergreen garland. Honey paused a second to take it all in. But only for a second because it was hard not to throw herself under the tree and grab her gift.

137

Just get the dress opened, and then she could see if it gave her the nerve to go to the Haunted Holiday Festival.

Everyone was already around the tree. Harvest was busy stacking and re-stacking the five packages, hoping to be the closest one when Dad, who was wearing a Santa hat gave the order to unwrap.

"Finally," Harry said. "What've you been doing? Carving your and Scooter's initials in your closet door?"

"Guess who picked me up from practice this week," Honey said. "Sarah Sinclair. Don't believe she mentioned you at all."

That was all it took to shut Harry up. One mention of Sarah's name and he wouldn't be able to speak until New Years.

"You two," said Mary. "Behave yourselves. It's time for presents."

138

The way Mom's eyes shone, Honey thought she must be really excited about what she was getting, but even after she opened her new purse, she still looked just as excited. Could it be that she was happier giving the presents away than getting one?

Dad unwrapped a new gearshift knob for Emma, the MG-F convertible he was restoring.

"Just what I wanted," he said looking at Mary. "How did you know?"

"A little birdy told me," Mary said with a wink.

"More likely the catalog pages Dad left lying around the house," Harry said.

"Yeah, you even circled the knob with red Sharpie, Dad. Come on," Honey said.

"So I'm not subtle," John Moon said.

Next, Mary Moon handed Harry a flat package in shiny silver paper.

"For me?" He tried to act cool, but he was as restless as Harvest. Harry removed the paper, opened the box, and stared at the wrapping inside. "It's from Bride of Frankenstein?"

Honey rose to her knees. Had Mom given him the wrong present? But Mom nodded. Something wasn't right. Harry lifted the plastic sleeve off the hanger and shook out a flash of yellow satin.

"It's a new cape!" he said. "This will be perfect for my magic show!"

139

Honey rubbed her eyes as Harry took it off the hanger. The yellow satin was only the lining. Tied around his neck, the black caught the light and looked like something alive. How funny that they were both getting things from the same store.

Mom presented Honey with the next gift

wrapped in blue paper dotted with tiny green trees. Honey couldn't help but look at the size of Harry's box. Did he get a yellow-lined cape to match her dress? Maybe she was going to be Harry's assistant. She bit her lip. She would have a matching dress for the stage. He'd never let her on stage before, but with their matching costumes, it'd look perfect. She'd know exactly how to do everything. She'd even be better than Sarah.

The paper ripped and the tape broke with a pop. Honey forced the box open, but instead of touching soft satin, she felt something lumpy. The bright colors looked more at home in a preschool than a formal clothing store. Then she saw the horrible head. Googly eyes caught hers. Every spot on the turtle shell was a different color and the bald turtle head reflected the Christmas tree lights.

141

False alarm.

She closed the box and grimaced. "This isn't my present. This is for Harvest."

Her mother's smile hardened. "No, it's for you."

"Mom," Honey leaned forward. "It's the T-U-R-T-L-E. It's for Harvest."

Her dad turned to mom with a questioning look.

"No, dear," Mary said. "What would Harvest need with a backpack? We noticed that your book bag is looking shabby. Time for a new one, and this one just spoke your name."

Honey stared at the turtle in silent horror. Unless her name was Nerdy Turtle Girl, there was a mistake. Then she darted a look at the fabulous cape Harry was flying around the room in. This could not possibly be happening.

"What is Harvest getting?" she asked.

"What's that have to do with it?" Mary asked.

Honey dropped the backpack. "I'll trade him. I don't care what it is, it can't be worse.

142

Mom, I'm in fifth grade." Nothing about this Christmas was going right. Not one single thing. She stood to go, trying very hard not to cry.

"Honey," her dad said. "You will pick up your gift, take it to your room and you will give your mom a hug before you leave. You might be disappointed, but mom thought long and hard about that gift."

How could Mom think that Honey, her ten-year-old daughter, wanted a preschool turtle backpack? She would never carry it. Never. After obeying her father, Honey stomped upstairs to her room. She slammed the door, threw the turtle against the wall, and flopped on her bed.

143

Worst.

Christmas.

Ever.

Why did she have to be the little sister of

a celebrity who gets a splendiferous new cape? Why couldn't she have a normal Christmas and not a spooky one? Why did she have to live in Sleepy Hollow?

Because that's where you are needed.

Honey lifted her head. Where had that voice come from? Great! Now she was going crazy. Besides, no one needed her. If she wasn't here, Becky and Claire could be friends without her. Reverend Allen wouldn't have to answer the phone when he was on vacation. Harvest could keep the disgusting turtle backpack and Harry would go along being good and famous.

We go where we are needed. You are here because you are needed.

Honey turned to the turtle, but it only looked back with those big googly eyes that seemed to see everything. Was it talking to her? No way. But Honey wouldn't let anyone or anything get the last word.

"I tried to bring the holiday back to Sleepy

Hollow. I tried to remind everyone the reason for this season. It's not Halloween. Every night does not have to be Halloween. I did everything I could. I even tried to get the bells to ring, but they were stolen and no one even cares. Everyone is busy with their own Halloween stuff. They won't listen to me because they think I am just a kid when I tell them that there could be something bigger. Something grander."

Show them.

She wasn't a magician. That was Harry's talent. All she had was a fighting personality and a strong sense of right versus wrong.

Be there.

Even if she was upset? Even if she was the only one who wanted something different? Even if she was alone?

You are never alone.

Honey looked at the ugly turtle again.

It hadn't moved. Nothing had moved, but everything had changed. This was the night the world celebrated the homecoming of its Master. The last night that darkness would rule unchallenged. This was not a night for her to hide. It was the time for light, and darkness only made the light shine brighter.

She would go to the Haunted Holiday Festival.

THEIR OLD, FAMILIAR CAROLS PLAY

"It's Christmas Eve," Honey whispered. "It's Christmas Eve." She kept her hands crammed in her pockets to stay warm, and to stop their shivering. The vampire Santa statue stood at the main entrance beneath the banner that read "Welcome to the

Sleepy Hollow Haunted Holiday Festival." She kept her eyes down, not looking at his face and trying not to notice his blood-stained gloves.

"You are a blockhead!" she said as she passed the statue.

"ARRRGGGHHHH!"

Honey jumped and covered her eyes. Her heart had nearly stopped, but now it was racing. At the sound of laughter, she braved a peek. It was Scooter dressed like an evil elf, or a troll with warts and moles that had tufts of hair sticking out of an almost bald, pimply head.

"Scared you!" he called.

Honey pulled herself up to her full height. She would not let Scooter and his stupid prank get the best of her. She assumed her warrior attitude.

"I helped you with your paper. Why are you being mean?"

148

"Because it's the Haunted Holiday Festival," Scooter said. "It's what you're supposed to do. Scare people."

"It's Christmas Eve," she said. "You don't scare people on Christmas Eve."

"Ooooo sorry, Your Highness. We do here."

She was over him. So over him. "Leave me alone," she said. He wasn't cute anymore. And he didn't even write good essays.

149

Honey wandered into the green and walked among the tents with shoulders hunched. Everyone wore Halloween costumes, most with a red ribbon or tinsel added for some lame Christmas effect, but they were still grotesque. Here and there she saw kids from her class, but the choir wasn't singing yet. She didn't recognize most of the people. She assumed they were strangers. Probably tourists wanting to get scared on Christmas. Well, they sure came to the right place.

A huge Christmas tree decorated with

spiders, bats, and bones stood in front of the clock tower. A punch bowl flickered with weird lights, and strange smoke poured out of it. Honey stood by the cookie table. The sugar cookies looked good, but on closer inspection the angels looked more like something from Doctor Who than the nativity. Something rustled at her side. It was Brianna.

Naturally, Brianna was in costume — she always was — but instead of coming up with something scary, she wore her angel costume from the play. Somehow, despite all her hot-glued additions, it looked simple and clean and bright amid the dark, frightening monsters. Brianna's hair had been put up in a bun with a few long curls escaping. Her mother must have helped her, because Honey had seen Brianna's art projects. For all her creativity, Brianna drew worse than two-year-old Harvest. Something about her coordination is what the mothers told the kids. And they'd definitely noticed in gym class, too. But she looked like a real angel tonight. A safe place in the middle of a brewing storm.

Brianna picked up a cookie. She sniffed it, then held it away as she studied the snarling angel. One long look at the cookie, then another down at her dress. She frowned, put the cookie back on the table, and walked away.

For Honey, the cookies no longer looked delicious. And not because Brianna put one back on the table after smelling it, either. They just didn't have any appeal. Honey didn't know why she was there, but she felt like she needed to come. Just then she saw a black car whiz past the green down Main Street. It had an odd, golden hood ornament that if Honey was seeing correctly had been broken. On the license plate were the words *We Drive By Night*. She shivered but not because of the cold.

151

She walked among the different vendors, games and societies sponsoring the party, and looked for any sign of truth. Was anyone else waiting like she was? Looking for something? Or maybe they were hiding.

The music blared. Screams of laughter, as

people were startled. Nothing wrong with having fun, Honey told herself. And yet, something was missing. Something was being deliberately suppressed and it took a lot of darkness to hide it. No amount of special effects could cover the void.

She came at last to the gingerbread house, and that's where she found Becky and Claire. Honey couldn't stop looking at Claire's awful dripping snowman outfit. And she couldn't help but notice the edible bones now being offered from the once innocent gingerbread house. Claire and Becky broke off skeleton pieces and nibbled like mice.

"Hey, guys," Honey said.

"This is so good." Claire didn't even look at her. She broke off a chunk of clavicle.

"MMM... the best candy in the world," Becky agreed. Becky had a licorice stick in one hand and a handful of Skittles in the other. At least her pony costume wasn't scary.

152

"You don't even like licorice," Honey said.

"This is different." Becky crammed the licorice in her mouth and pulled another strip off the fake shutters. Her hoof mittens were getting sticky.

"Here, have some." Claire plucked a cone of cotton-candy off a bush that was planted beneath the window.

It had to be sweet to cover what was missing.

153

"No, thanks," Honey said. "I guess you noticed I'm not wearing a beautiful yellow satin gown."

But they hadn't. They were having fun without her.

Pointy-toed boots emerged in the doorway. Honey recognized the woman who'd been decorating earlier that week, only this time she was dressed as a witch with a piece of mistletoe stuck in her black hat. "Yes, have some candy," she said. "Or you can come inside when you're ready. I think your friends are about ready."

The way her eyes looked them over gave Honey chills. She couldn't remember a witch at a Christmas gingerbread house. She stepped back and looked at the house again. This wasn't a winter story. It was Hansel and Gretel, and her friends were eating like pigs.

"Let's go," she said. Didn't Becky and Claire know how Hansel and Gretel ended? She had to get them out of there. "Don't you have to sing in the school choir?"

Claire shrugged. "Not worried about it."

"Come on," Honey said. "With your voice, you probably need the extra credit to pass the class."

Becky chewed on the licorice. "We don't have to sing for another hour. We have a lot of time."

An hour? Honey looked around her. People bumping into each other, shoving at a game to get first pick over the prizes. The emcee was announcing the winners of the scariest nutcracker award. She couldn't last another hour. Becky and Claire didn't seem to feel the same darkness she felt. They didn't understand. With the Christmas play now canceled, Honey had no choice but to stay and sing with the school choir. She couldn't face this alone. A child cried as a mean dog on a leash barked. People booed at the unpopular choice of winner at the nutcracker contest. All the noise, the clamor, all of this going on instead of a silent, peaceful night. All she wanted was a normal Christmas, something people expected. Not this.

155

Christmas should never be normal. Christmas is miraculous.

Honey opened her eyes. What did that mean? What was wrong with a simple, normal Christmas? Becky and Claire were still eating. "Did you hear that?" she asked them.

They shook their heads. A cool breeze blew through. The flaps of the tents snapped.

The music from the emcee grew louder. Honey was just about to cover them when she heard it again.

"Listen," she said. She spun and looked up. "Listen. Do you hear it?"

"Hear what?" Claire gnawed on a dagger-shaped candy cane.

It was unmistakable now . . . and growing louder. And not just one of them, but a whole chorus. If Honey had to guess, she'd say twelve tones.

"It's the bells," she cried. "The bells are ringing."

Claire lowered the dagger. "That's impossible."

"I hear them!" Becky's face lit up as she dropped the candy and moved toward the edge of the lot.

Now others were hearing them, too. Voices hushed. The music from the speakers faded, and eyes turned toward the sky where the steeple was outlined against the moon. Louder and louder they rang, clanging, chiming. The ground trembled beneath Honey's feet. She felt the bells in her chest almost like the booms of fireworks.

"Who's ringing them?" Claire yelled, and even then, Honey could barely hear her. Their song sped over the roofs of Sleepy Hollow, down into the alleys and across the fields, and raced over the bay. The Haunted Holiday Festival had grown strangely quiet. People moved out of the green and onto the church grounds. This was no normal Christmas at all. Miraculous was the only way to describe it.

"They are beautiful," Jack-o-Lantern Frost yelled.

"I haven't heard them for years," the Psychotic Nutcracker admitted.

Twelve bells, Honey thought. *Who? And how? The North Church bell tower is empty.* She had seen with her own eyes. This was the sound of Christmas itself, an ancient sound that'd pealed for two thousand years. That was the song filling the emptiness.

Slowly the music began to calm to a rhythmic lullaby, and there stood Brianna on the church steps in her angel costume, her eyes shining like she'd just seen a miracle.

Her voice wasn't super clear, but it seemed to carry on the strength of the bells.

"And in despair I bowed my head.
'There is no peace on earth,' I said,
'For hate is strong and mocks the song
Of peace on earth, good will to men.

"Then pealed the bells more loud and deep:
'God is not dead, nor doth He sleep;
The wrong shall fail, the right prevail
With peace on earth, good will to men.'

"How does she know all that?" asked Claire.

"She remembers everything she hears," said Becky.

Brianna finished her song, then without any fanfare she turned away from the crowd. Instead of waiting for applause or recognition, she started home through the neighborhood —a pretty blond girl in white with a skip in her step.

The music faded. Calm settled on the crowd like a cool, satin sheet. A hoot owl could be heard back at the town square. And was that a cow mooing from Folly Farm?

159

"That was some sound system," another scary Santa said. "Well, they had their moment. Let's get back to the festival." Spreading his arms wide he walked toward the gate of the Haunted Holiday Festival as if herding sheep. Some turned and made their way back to the festival, but many stayed where they were, gazing into the star-studded sky, searching for the fading pealing of the bells.

"That was unbelievable." It was Miss Fortissimo. She took out a pair of vampire teeth so she could talk more clearly. "That performance earned you bonus points, Honey

Moon, even without singing tonight."

"It wasn't me," Honey said, but her voice was drowned out by the crowd.

"I hadn't realized how I missed the bells. I wonder if they ever got the repairs finished." A man dressed like the Grinch pulled out his wallet. "I meant to donate back then."

Honey pulled Becky to her. "Did you hear that? Maybe we'll get enough to replace the bells!"

160

"It's worth a shot, Honey," she said. "But where did the music come from?"

A man with a hideous, furry face scratched at the hair glued on his cheek. "The belfry is empty. I know it is. We took...." His eyes shot over to Honey. "Hey, you're his sister, aren't you? That magic kid?"

"Did you hear the music?" Honey asked him. Now Becky and Claire stood shoulder to shoulder with her. "Wasn't it marvelous?"

He studied the three of them warily. "Yeah, marvelous. And I don't know where they hid their speakers, either. I'll talk to the mayor about that. Probably against a city ordinance."

Honey could only smile. No ordinance on paper could stand against the power that'd quaked the earth that night. An arrival. A reclaiming, like the trumpet blast when a king takes his throne. For one night, Halloween had met its match.

161

All this time Honey had been longing for a normal Christmas—Santa, carols, trees with lights and tinsel. Now she understood that those traditions were fun, but they weren't strong enough to hold back the darkness. It wasn't a normal Christmas that would fill the hole in Sleepy Hollow. It was something stronger than that. It was in the heart of every man or woman, boy or girl who loved what was good and right. That's what would eventually win the fight against Halloween.

I go where I am needed.

Honey Moon had found where she was needed.

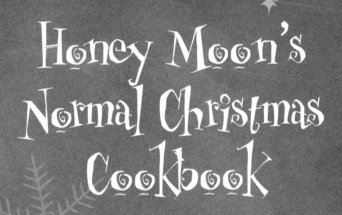

Honey Moon's
Normal Christmas
Cookbook

Hi Girlfriend,

Thanks for coming along on my Christmas adventure. I got to say, I'm kind of glad it's over but even more glad that I got to hear the bells on Christmas Eve. Just between you and me, I was a little scared those steps in the bell tower might crash.

But what Christmas is complete without some cookies and fun craft ideas?

I've been hanging out in my room with Becky and Claire and we came up with some truly splendiferous goodies and crafts that are easy to bake and easy to make.

My favorite are the Peanut Butter Bells. Especially when they are still warm, just out of the oven and the chocolate is all soft and melty. Uhmm, I can taste them now.

I think even Brianna Royal would be thrilled with my snow globe craft. You know how she loves sequins and glitter. And Harry and his blockhead friends will devour my Blockhead Brownies.

So go ahead and turn the pages to find some ideas to brighten your holidays even more.

And thanks again for coming along and be sure to visit me on the web where you can share your ideas with me. How cool is that?

Love,

Honey

P.S. Remember: Always assemble all your ingredients, bowls and measuring spoons and cups before starting any recipe. There's a technical term for this. It's: *Mise en place*—that's a French culinary term which means, SET IN PLACE.

Oh, and if you need help in the kitchen be sure to ask.

Peanut Butter Bells

You might want to make extra. These go fast. And be careful, your brother or your sister might even hug you.

Ingredients:

1/2	cup granulated sugar
1	cup packed brown sugar
1	cup creamy peanut butter
1	cup butter or margarine, softened
2	eggs
3	cups all-purpose flour
1 1/2	teaspoons baking soda
1	teaspoon baking powder

Additional granulated sugar (about 2 tablespoons)

About 7 dozen chocolate bells. You can usually find them in the bulk candy section of the grocery store.

Directions:

- Heat oven to 375°F. In large bowl, beat 1/2 cup granulated sugar, the brown sugar, peanut butter, butter and eggs with electric mixer on medium speed, or mix with a big spoon. Stir in flour, baking soda and baking powder.

- Shape dough into 1-inch balls; roll in additional granulated sugar. Place about 2 inches apart on ungreased cookie sheet.

- Bake 8 to 10 minutes or until edges are light brown. Immediately press 1 chocolate bell in center of each cookie. Remove from cookie sheet to wire rack.

And try to save some for family and guests. They are scrumptious.

167

SUGAR BELLS

Now these are pretty easy. You can make your own cookie dough from scratch or use store bought, the kind in the tube is fine.

Don't forget: *Mise en place*

From Scratch

Ingredients:
Cookies
1 ½   cups powdered sugar
1   cup butter or margarine, softened
1   teaspoon vanilla

1/2   teaspoon almond extract (optional)
1   egg
2 ½   cups all-purpose flour
1   teaspoon baking soda
1   teaspoon cream of tartar
Plenty of candy sprinkles, nonpareils or colored sugars for decorating.

Icing:
2   cups powdered sugar
1/2   teaspoon vanilla
2   tablespoons milk or half-and-half

Directions:

- In large bowl, mix 1 1/2 cups powdered sugar, the butter, 1 teaspoon vanilla, almond extract and egg until well blended. Stir in flour, baking soda and cream of tartar. <u>Cover and refrigerate at least 3 hours</u>. Now you can take a break and go read a book or go outside and play.

- Heat oven to 375°F. Divide dough in half. On lightly floured, cloth covered surface, roll each half of dough 3/16 (or so—doesn't have to be exact) inch thick. Cut into bell shapes with your cookie cutter. Oh, I almost forgot, if cookies are to be hung as decorations, make a hole in each 1/4 inch from top with end of plastic straw. Place on ungreased cookie sheet.

- 3 Bake 7 to 8 minutes or until light brown. Remove from cookie sheet to cooling rack. Cool completely, about 30 minutes.

- 4 In medium bowl, beat all frosting ingredients until smooth and spreadable. Tint with food color if desired. Frost and decorate cookies as desired with frosting and colored sugars.

169

SUGAR BELLS (Not from Scratch)

These are easy and quick. Good if you ever have a cookie emergency. Hey, it could happen.

Open up the tube of cookie dough. Break the log in half and then roll out on a floured surface.

Easy peasy, right?

Then just cut out your bells. Bake according to the package directions and decorate with colored sugars or icing.

Here's a recipe that my mother told me has been in our family for years and years.

GINGERBREAD COOKIES

This is a great recipe for making gingerbread boys or girls. Or you can even use it to make a gingerbread house or maybe you can try and build the North Church Bell Tower. Wow!

This recipe is the best. And it makes your house smell good too — mmmmm.

170

Ingredients:

1   cup packed brown sugar
1/3   cup shortening
1 ½   cups dark molasses (It's sooooo sticky. Don't get it in your hair.)
2/3   cup cold water
7   cups all-purpose flour
2   teaspoons baking soda
2   teaspoons ground ginger
1   teaspoon ground allspice
1   teaspoon ground cloves
1   teaspoon ground cinnamon
1/2   teaspoon salt

I like to decorate my gingerbread boys and girls with raisin eyes and buttons and royal icing.

Directions:
- Mix brown sugar, shortening, molasses and water in large bowl. Stir in flour, baking soda, ginger, allspice, cloves, cinnamon and salt. Cover and refrigerate about 2 hours or until firm.

- Heat oven to 350°F. Grease cookie sheet lightly. Roll 1/4th of dough at a time 1/4 inch thick on floured surface. Cut with floured gingerbread cookie cutter or other favorite shaped cutter. I like to make gingerbread reindeer. Place about 2 inches apart on cookie sheet. Add raisins for eyes and buttons.

- Bake 10 to 12 minutes or until almost no indentation remains when touched in center. Immediately remove from cookie sheet. Cool on wire rack.

Frost cookies with royal icing and decorate however you want.

171

Royal Icing

1	1-lb box of 10X sugar
1 tsp	cream of tartar
3	egg whites

Put in a mixing bowl and use an electric mixer to beat ingredients until thick and shiny. Takes about 5 minutes. Put icing in a zip lock freezer bag and nip off one corner so you can pipe the icing out. Don't nip off too much or the icing will ooze out all over the place. This icing dries very quickly, so any you don't use should be stored in a plastic airtight container. It dries quick and hard, so it's good for "gluing" cookies together and putting on candy decorations.

172

Blockhead Brownies

This is an easy recipe for fudgy brownies. After they bake, cut them into large squares, about two-inches all around. Then use Royal Icing to draw funny faces on them. Fun!

Ingredients:
1/2   cup vegetable oil

1   cup sugar
1   teaspoon vanilla
2   large eggs
1/4   teaspoon baking powder
1/3   cup cocoa powder
1/4   teaspoon salt
1/2   cup all-purpose flour

Preheat oven to 350°.
Mix oil and sugar until well blended.
Add eggs and vanilla; stir just until blended.
Mix all dry ingredients in a separate bowl.
Stir dry ingredients into the oil/sugar mixture.
Pour into greased 9 x 9 square pan.
Bake for 20 minutes or until sides just start
    to pull away from the pan.
Cool completely before cutting.

173

Honey Note:
    This recipe can be doubled very easily. Just
double the ingredients and bake in a 9 x 13
pan. If you double the recipe, you will need to
cook longer than 20 minutes.

Dear Diary: _____

DEAR DIARY...

175

Dear Diary: _____

176

DEAR DIARY...

177

Dear Diary: _____

Dear Diary...

179

Dear Diary: _____

180

DEAR DIARY...

181

Dear Diary: _____

DEAR DIARY...

183

Dear Diary: _____

184

DEAR DIARY...

185

Dear Diary: _____

186

CREATOR'S NOTES

I am enchanted with the world of Honey Moon, the younger sister of Harry Moon. She is smart and courageous and willing to do anything to help right win out. What a powerhouse.

I wish I had a friend like Honey when I was in school. There is something cool about the way Honey and her friends connect with each other that's very special. When I was Honey's age, I spent most of my time in our family barn taking care of rabbits and didn't hang out with other kids a lot. I think I was always a little bit on the outside.

Maybe that's why I like Honey so much. She lives life with wonderful energy and enthusiasm. She doesn't hesitate to speak her mind. And she demands that adults pay attention to her because more often than not, the girl knows what she is talking about. And she often finds herself getting into all kinds of crazy adventures.

We all need real friends like Honey. Growing up is quite an adventure and living it with girlfriends that you love builds friendships that can last a lifetime. That's the point, I think, of Honey's enchanted world — life is just better when you work it out with friends.

I am happy that you have decided to join me along with author Regina Jennings in the enchanted world of Honey Moon. I would love for you to let us know about any fun ideas you have for Honey in her future stories. Visit harrymoon.com and let us know.

See you again in our next visit to the enchanted world of Honey Moon!

MARK ANTHONY POE

189

The Enchanted World of Honey Moon creator Mark Andrew Poe never thought about creating a town where kids battled right and wrong. His dream was to love and care for animals, specifically his friends in the rabbit community.

Along the way, Mark became successful in all sorts of interesting careers. He entered the print and publishing world as a young man and his company did really, really well. Mark also became a popular and nationally sought-after health care advocate for the care and well-being of rabbits.

Years ago, Mark came up with the idea of a story about a young boy with a special connection to a world of magic, all revealed through a remarkable rabbit friend. Mark worked on his idea for several years before building a collaborative creative team to help him bring his idea to life.

Harry Moon was born. The team was thrilled when Mark introduced Harry's enchanting sister, Honey Moon. Boy, did she pack an unexpected punch!

In 2014, Mark began a multi-book project to launch *The Amazing Adventures of Harry Moon* and *The Enchanted World of Honey Moon* into the youth marketplace. Harry and Honey are kids who understand the difference between right and wrong. Kids who tangle with magic and forces unseen in a town where "every day is Halloween night." Today, Mark continues to work on the many stories of Harry Moon. He lives in suburban Chicago with his wife and his 25 rabbits.

REGINA JENNINGS

Author Regina Jennings is a popular romance author living outside Oklahoma City with her husband and four kids. She is every bit as feisty as Honey Moon and claims to know her well.

191

BE SURE TO READ THE
CONTINUING AND ENCHANTED
ADVENTURES OF HONEY MOON.

HONEY MOON 🌑 BOOK CLUB

Become a member of the
Honey Moon Book Club and receive another
of Honey's adventures every other month
along with a bag full of goodies!

Skip over to **www.harrymoon.com**
and sign up today.

VISIT **HARRYMOON.COM** FOR
EVERYTHING HONEY, HARRY & THE LATEST NEWS

JOIN THE HONEY MOON BOOK CLUB

Each delighted reader receives these benefits:

1. **SIX hardcover editions** of *The Enchanted Adventures of Honey Moon.* That's a new book delivered every two months. *(3 books for 6 mo. subscribers)*

2. **SIX free e-book versions** of each new book (downloaded using our included Honey Moon smart phone and tablet app. *(3 books for 6 mo. subscribers)*

3. Your first book is delivered in a beautiful **Honey Moon Collectables Box**.

5. **Wall posters** of Honey and all her friends are on the inside of each book's dust jacket—images straight from the Sleepy Hollow Portrait Gallery.

6. The very popular and useful **monogramed drawstring backpack** from the Sleepy Hollow Outfitters store.

7. From the Sleepy Hollow Magic Store a **pouch of magical fragrances** transporting you to the town's aromas.

8. The large 15" x 21" **Fun Map of Sleepy Hollow**—takes you everywhere around town.

9. A **special edition** of the *Sleepy Hollow Gazette*, including a welcome from the mayor and stories about the upcoming books and not-to-miss events. PLUS, you receive monthly editions of the *Sleepy Hollor Gazette* via email and the app.

10. Plus, if you choose, the Collectables Box will also include the **golden Sleepy Hollow Outfitters carabiner**. Very handy.

11. And a second optional choice is to include the very cool **Honey Moon monogramed knit beanie**.

Total value of this package - $215 (plus optional items 10 and 11)